Professor Hanaa

Reem Bassiouney

Translated from the Arabic by Dr Laila Helmi

Garnet Publishing

PROFESSOR HANAA

Published by
Garnet Publishing Limited
8 Southern Court
South Street
Reading
RG1 4QS
UK

www.garnetpublishing.co.uk
www.twitter.com/Garnetpub
www.facebook.com/Garnetpub
garnetpub.wordpress.com

First Edition

ISBN: 978-1-85964-272-6

British Library Cataloguing-in-Publication Data
A catalogue record for this book is available from the British Library

Typeset by Samantha Barden
Jacket design by Garnet Publishing
Cover photograph © Reg Charity/CORBIS

Printed and bound in Lebanon by International Press:
interpress@int-press.com

*'Men have had every advantage of us in telling their own story ...
the pen has been in their hands.'*

Jane Austen

To every Middle Eastern woman who holds a pen to write her own story.
Whatever type of pen!
For hers is the honour of trying.

And to every Egyptian who loves passionately, hates passionately
and enjoys Middle Eastern pastries.

Chapter 1

There are days in life that are quiet and dull, and others that pass in a rush of ecstasy. There are days full of indolence, of restlessness. And then there are days ... oh God!

This day in particular seemed endless and depressing, even more so than usual, because today was her birthday. Her fortieth.

Twenty years ago she had vowed that on her fortieth birthday, she would throw a huge party and invite her husband, his relatives and her children's friends, that she would extend the invitation to all officers and employees, to housewives and all those in authority, to decision-makers and self-made men – and to all workers and peasants.

The day had come, but Hanaa was alone in her spinster's den, and as solitary as a wild cat.

Spinster. What an awful, terrifying word!

She was not a spinster and did not look like forty at all. Looking at herself in the mirror, she looked like thirty; twenty perhaps. She was still petite, and her wrists slender and fragile. How does a woman grow old? When her wrist loses the charm of youth. But *her* wrist was full of charm. Her small, sharp features had not changed; they were still like those of a little squirrel. Her figure had not lost its grace. Even the faint wrinkles around her eyes were hardly visible.

It was a well-planned but unsettling day, and despite her courage she hardly knew how to face it. Still, she managed to stay organized as usual, and wrote down her plans for the day.

At nine, she would visit her former professor, who had suffered a light stroke, in hospital. After that, she would try once more to meet with her department head, and finally she had to prepare to travel to the conference the next day.

Only one thing possessed her: one idea nagged at her mind.

She would go to the head of the department while still a virgin.

She would prepare for the conference while still a virgin.

She would turn forty while still a virgin.

The very idea filled her with disgust. There had to be a way out. Her virginity was strangling her, wrestling her to the ground. Her virginity, which she had guarded so jealously for years now, had become her arch enemy. Who was worthy of deflowering Professor Hanaa? Had that man been born yet?

One single idea possessed her: today, she had to lose her virginity – fast – or else she would become a bitter, forty-year-old spinster. If on the other hand she were to lose her virginity, she would turn into a *woman* of forty. That was something to be proud of … whereas to remain a girl at forty, because he who deserved her had not yet been born? That was simply a catastrophe. Fortunately, she was practically minded, and knew exactly what she wanted.[1]

---

1 In Egypt, as in many other Middle Eastern and Arab countries, a girl has to guard her virginity until she is married. Virginity for a girl reflects not just her honour but the honour of her family as well. So if a girl loses her virginity before marriage, that may bring shame to all her immediate and even distant family and may also mean that her sisters will never get married. That may also explain why families ask for a dowry, a secured flat and expensive gifts for their daughters from their bridegroom-to-be. Because the man and his family have to save for years in order to marry, he expects his bride to be a virgin. This also means that girls prepare for the day of their wedding long beforehand, since it really marks their initiation into womanhood and into a different phase of their life, one with perhaps more status and pride attached.

Professor Hanaa Saad sat in the anteroom, irritated, watching the department secretary, Mr Abdel Hamid, with an uncommonly intense feeling of anticipation and rage. He was a middle-aged man, always wearing his fake leather jacket and his almost-too-tight grey trousers. His thinning hair wasn't any particular colour and his thick fish lips were mostly either smacking wordlessly or jabbering nonsense. If she had one desire today, it was to smash Mr Abdel Hamid's head with a heavy but sharp hammer until she felt his blood spurting, dripping down her hands, nose and eyes.

'Professor Hanaa, I already told you that Professor Samy is very busy today,' he said, in the tone of Caliph al-Hakim bi-Amr Allah on the day he banned green soup and set fire to the streets of Cairo.

Heaving a deep sigh, her voice harsh and shaky, she insisted, 'He has to sign the consent for my travelling today. If he doesn't, I can't go to the conference and if I don't—'

'Professor Hanaa, I said he was busy!' he interrupted, peeved. He turned away contemptuously and started talking to another professor. She was not ready to give up, though. She had to travel tomorrow. Today she had to lose her virginity, get her own back on that secretary and rip her rights out from the very jaws of the beast.

This was the age of ripping, the age of Abdel Hamid and of fear, hypocrisy and indolence, the age of zealots and colonialists. It was an age she hated, an atmosphere she did not know, and the secretary turned her stomach.

She closed her eyes, listening to the flattery heaped upon the secretary by all the university professors seeking the head of the department's approval.

How long had she been sitting there? How long had she stayed?

Finally she heard the secretary's powerful voice. 'Professor Hanaa, Professor Samy wants to see you.'

She got up, moving steadily in her flowing dress with her black hair and unusual orange sandals. Confidently, she opened the door and looked at her colleague, who excelled in hypocrisy and public relations. The head of the department! She hated Samy; she hated his wife and his son, the teaching assistant; she hated his whole family, who worked at the university. She hated Samy the professor and Samy the man.

The feeling was mutual.

She examined his dyed-brown eyebrows and hair, his velvet tie and brown suit, his long pale face and phantom-like figure. He looked like Caspar in Dickens' *A Tale of Two Cities,* except thirty years older and much more vulgar.

Sarcastically he asked, 'So, Hanaa, you want to go to America?'

He called her Hanaa when she had to call him Professor Samy! She hated calling him 'Professor Samy'.

Frostily she said, 'I want permission to attend the conference. I asked for it three months ago and you still haven't approved it. Why?'

'I ask, you answer. Not the other way around,' he said brusquely.

She felt the blood boiling in her veins. 'No. I am asking,' she said forcefully.

He looked at the pile of exam papers in front of him. 'You haven't marked your exams. I could have you up for questioning.'

With every inch of her body trembling, she said vehemently, 'I did not mark those papers because I did not teach that subject. You know that. Professor Ali taught it and then left for a teaching post in Saudi Arabia. You approved his secondment, yet you won't approve my attending an academic conference that will help me with—'

He interrupted her firmly. 'Did you say "you"? Sir! You mean "Sir"! Look, Hanaa, you either mark the exams or I will not give my consent to you travelling.'

She started to open her mouth, but he went on. 'I haven't got time to waste. You have five hundred papers. Can you have them marked by tomorrow morning? If you can, I'll sign the consent. You'll sign for the papers and hand them in to Abdel Hamid in the morning.'

She looked at him in amazement and horror, despair creeping into her brain while ideas accumulated within her.

Her fortieth birthday and still a virgin!

Tomorrow she would go to America, where her first love lived: Ramy el-Masry.

Today she must lose her virginity, mark five hundred papers, slap Samy soundly, then smash Abdel Hamid's head with a hammer. Lose her virginity, go to the conference and perhaps meet Ramy, perhaps not.

Lose her virginity.

She would go back home then.

Once again she sat there staring at Abdel Hamid. With five hundred papers in her lap she could hardly see his face.

'Professor Hanaa.'

Through the papers she saw a young man standing in front of her. 'How are you, Khaled?' she asked mechanically.

He smiled, his eyes never meeting hers. 'Do you need help, professor? Shall I carry those papers for you?'

'Oh would you, please?' she asked, struggling to get up.

He took the papers from her. She got up and moved towards the door, without uttering a word to Abdel Hamid.

Walking next to the young man, she looked at him. Her eyes travelled all the way up to his head. He was tall, dark and slim. He was a typical Egyptian and his eyes never met hers; shyness emanated from every feature and confidence glittered between his lips. She needed a man. Khaled was no older than twenty-five or-six and she was forty. But she was small and slight and she always quickly got rid of the grey hairs with a strong black dye that matched her thick black eyebrows.

'Where to?' he asked calmly.

'Khaled, did you want to see Professor Samy? I'm sorry I've taken you from—'

'I'll go back to him in an hour,' he quietly interrupted. 'Do you need help, professor?'

She looked into his eyes, but he shyly averted them. Smiling, she said, 'I need a lot of help. A *lot* of help.'

In that same quiet voice that she found so provoking he said, 'Happy to be of service.'

'Thanks, Khaled. Remember when I used to teach you Victorian poetry? You were my best student.'

'You're just being kind.'

Khaled was an exemplary student. He was obedient and helpful, a hard and diligent worker, and he was poor. She could discern his poverty in his hobbies, his constant work, his embitterment with the wealthy, his sometimes straightforward way of expressing himself and his sophisticated way of avoiding conflicts.

Happily she chirped, 'Could you help me mark these papers? You know I have a conference tomorrow and if I don't finish grading all these, I can't go.'

'Of course, professor,' he said without hesitating. 'Anything you want. Leave me half of them. I'll stay up and do them.'

'No!' she hastily said. 'This is a responsibility. You have to mark them in my presence. I'm sorry – I know you're being helpful. Could you come and mark them at my place?'

There was something like fear in the look he gave her. 'If you leave them, I—'

'Khaled,' she interrupted, 'I can't leave them. I'm only asking you to mark them at my place. I'm not going to be alone there.'

He heaved a sigh of relief. 'I'm sorry, I thought you – of course I'll come. Is after sunset prayers OK? I have a few errands to run.'

'Oh, that's great!' she said triumphantly.

She switched the lights on in the large hall and threw the exam papers on the table. Her house was old; it was her parents' house. Here she had lost them both. Here she would spend the rest of her life, perhaps alone. Perhaps not. Here she had lived for most of her forty years. She loved her home; she had acquired certain habits she could not live without. As opposed to her sister, she was economical with the electricity. She kept the lights switched off till seven o'clock every evening. At seven she would switch on only the light in her room, where she would sip her coffee and read. Before she slept, she would open the large window in her bedroom and take a deep breath of air, looking down at the crowded streets of Zamalek. She would drink the camomile tea some people had recommended and which she had been drinking since the death of her mother ten years ago. She would then go to bed, craving sleep the way a man craves the woman he loves. Sometimes sleep came. Other times it did not.

Professor Hanaa was neat and cautious. Everything in the kitchen had its place. She only ate sweet stuff when she visited her sister. She only ate meat once a week and although she loved grilled meat, she hated grilling it. She would buy it from a kebab shop then go through the process of cleaning it, which usually took an hour. Since she ate her main meal at six o'clock in the evening, she had to plan to buy the grilled meat early.

The cleaning started with her getting rid of the tahini paste, the salad and the bread. The meat was then placed in the oven for half an hour after the minute specks of parsley scattered on the meat had been carefully picked off.

Professor Hanaa did not like visits, especially those from her family. She could see the greed in her brother's eyes and the worry in her sister's. She hated both greed and worrying.

Her kitchen was the same as her mother had left it ten years ago. It was clean and the food in the house was scanty and nutritious. There was carefully prepared salad, frozen soup, frozen fish, and there was the chicken breast that she ate on Thursdays after work.

She picked up her own particular cup and calmly started to prepare her coffee, her older sister's words ringing in her head.

Hanaa. No men and no food. What are you living for?! Those are the pleasures of life!

She glanced proudly at her slender wrist. She was beautiful; that was enough! She had to remain beautiful, graceful, small, slim, and would anyone remember her fortieth birthday?

What did she know about Khaled? She knew he lived in Boulaq. He often mentioned the fact with an air of pride. He was self-confident but his eyes never met those of a woman. Was he a virgin, too? What else did she know? She knew he was religious; he never forgot to pray. She knew he was an exemplary student, and that his best friend was a blind young man whom Khaled helped with everything. Khaled was an example of the kind, patient Egyptian. He had been top of his class, got a place at the university as a teaching assistant and was awarded an MA in the translation of the Holy Quran. And he was a man, he was young – and that was what she wanted.

She sat quietly, drinking her coffee and staring at the black clock on the wall. Her mind was focused on one problem. Khaled was religious. What could she expect of him? What about herself? She believed in God, but she had a strange sense of frustration and exasperation that she had never felt before. She saw no crime in losing her virginity. Chastity may be a source of pride at twenty and an ornament at thirty; but at forty, it was nothing but a curse! Enough of chastity! What had chastity done for her? Did she know the scent of a man? The touch of a man? What did she know about men?

Ramy had never so much as touched her! What was wrong with the men in Egypt? Were they afraid of women? What was so frightening about a woman? Why so much thought? Why so much gallantry? Why hadn't she lost her virginity in all this time? Why hadn't she forgotten Ramy like he had forgotten her? Why had her life gone to waste over work, study, fear and an impossible love?

She had been stupid, but now the age of stupidity was over.

She had been lazy, but now the age of laziness was over.

Once she had lost her virginity – what would she do then? Celebrate and celebrate. Throw all constraint into the River Nile, for spinsters never get married. Spinsters are a shame to society. Men don't marry forty-year-old spinsters, only widows or divorcees. After losing her virginity, she would throw a great party and invite Professor Samy, Abdel Hamid, her brother, her sister, the porter, Nagat the maid, and maybe—

She clasped her stomach. Maybe it was time for this sleeping womb to awaken and for these wasted ovaries to be fertilized. Perhaps it was time the woman within rebelled and overthrew the respectable lecturer!

Perhaps it was time this bedroom became inflamed and throbbing.

Perhaps.

Khaled was religious. She knew nothing about him. He might be in a relationship. Maybe he found her old, jaded. Maybe.

She had never tried to seduce a man before – no man. Then why didn't she hate men? Why hadn't she decided that men were a blight on society? If she hated men, she could accept things as they were, the way her professor had before her. If only she hated men! But did she even really know them?

Today she would know everything there was to know about men. Everything, and from a reliable source!

She must not, however, forget that she had five hundred papers to be marked and that seducing someone like Khaled would not be easy.

She must think of all the strategies she had read about. Her own life was meagre, her experience deplorably wanting. How was she to seduce him?

She did not want to seduce him; she wanted him to penetrate that obstacle that stood between her and her femininity. She did not want to seduce him at all.

She remembered how, in *A Passage to India,* the English girl had gone into the caves with the Indian man, and then had accused him of raping her. She had not been sure of what took place in the cave. She taught the novel to the fourth year, and Khaled had been one of her students. 'I don't understand this novel,' he had said in amazement. 'Does the author really mean that the English girl doesn't remember an incident like that? That's rubbish. These things are unforgettable.'

She, on the other hand, believed the girl. She thought it was easy for the mind to be intoxicated without having a drink. It is easy for the mind to lose control without resorting to hallucinogenic drugs. Every mind has its key, its weak spot, and is susceptible to delirium.

She was older than Khaled, more intelligent. She – well, she had to mark five hundred papers, she needed to lose her virginity, then she needed to wake up early tomorrow to go to America. She needed to awaken her dormant womb and to revenge herself on Samy and Abdel Hamid and all those who had power and authority as well as all those who served them.

Khaled stood shyly and hesitantly at the door, still wearing his dark blue jeans and checked shirt. It did not seem as if he had had the time to go home. Good. This would make her mission easier. She needed him tired enough to lose control and aroused enough to act upon it. She was also still wearing the same clothes, formal and modest, so as not to raise his doubts.

Quickly she said, 'Do come in, Khaled.'

He came in quietly, and she gestured for him to take a seat. No sooner did he sit down than he asked, in a serious tone, 'Shall we start grading now?'

He looked at her and she understood the unspoken question. Though not used to lying, she said confidently, 'Nagat the maid is inside, if you want anything.'

He calmed down somewhat and they started grading at the long table.

She looked at him while he focused on the grading. He worked diligently. His features were even and his steady dark eyes were now concentrating on the task at hand. He seemed to radiate an air of patience all around him.

She put down the pen and said, 'I don't know how to thank you.'

Without looking up at her he replied, 'Always at your service, professor.'

Hastily she continued, 'Do you have brothers and sisters?'

'A brother and a sister.'

'Exactly like me. Are they married?'

'My younger brother got engaged two months ago. My sister is at school.'

'And you?' she asked nonchalantly.

Still crouched over the exams, he said, 'I was in a committed relationship until about a year ago, but—'

'Your colleague at the university!' she blurted out.

He looked up at her suddenly, rather surprised. Professor Hanaa was not reputed to be curious. On the contrary, she was known to be strict about everything, particularly about marks and forms of conduct. She was finicky, complex and out of touch with the real world. She seemed not to care about other people's lives, yet he admired her sense of morality and conscientiousness. She disapproved of favouritism and worked hard. He would never have imagined that one day he would be at her home, and that she would ask him about his life quite so bluntly. He glanced at his watch. It was eleven. Hesitantly he said, 'It's getting late. I can take the papers with me and bring them back tomorrow morning. I'll stay up all night doing them.'

It was a mistake to have asked him about his life! There she was, already blundering. Quickly, she refused. 'No, no you can't.'

He wanted to reply, but she said forcefully, 'If you're tired, you can leave; I'll try to get it done on my own.' There was a moment of silence. She held her breath.

What if he left?

She had to appear strong and confident.

What if he agreed?

Before he could utter a word, she added, 'I'm sorry Khaled. I thought you were a student of mine and you wouldn't hesitate to come to my home.'

'I'll stay for an hour,' he replied firmly.

'Are you afraid of the doorman?' she inquired in a challenging tone. 'Everybody knows you're my student and that we work together.'

'I can't stay here, professor. It's not appropriate.'

He burst out without thinking, 'It's inappropriate, and it's against religion for me to stay in your flat in the middle of the night. It's *harām*.'

She got up, her cheeks flushed. 'Do you want tea or coffee?'

She knew what people would think if they found out that he was in her flat in the middle of the night. But she had to stay in control and not lose her temper.

'Oh – tea would be lovely, with three spoonfuls of sugar.'

'I don't have sugar. I never use any.'

He smiled slightly. 'You're the complete opposite of my mother. If there was no sugar at our house, she would declare war on us all.'

He had once again begun to lose his reserve, and she did not want to speak. She was scared of uttering a word that might scare him. She wanted his mind to be intoxicated. It would not be for hours yet. She wanted him to become so absorbed in grading that he lost track of time.

Time passed. The more it passed, the more hopeful she got.

Suddenly she said, 'Do you think helping me is *harām*? I mean, is it exploitation to have you mark exams that I'm supposed to do?'

He smiled. It was the first time she had ever seen him smile. It was an innocent and calm smile. 'But this is not your subject,' he said. 'This is Professor Ali's subject and he's gone abroad, so it doesn't matter who marks it.'

'What do you think of Professor Samy?'

'A charlatan.'

'I beg your pardon?'

'You wanted my opinion.'

'You don't like him?'

'He's a charlatan and I don't like charlatans.'

'And Professor Ali?'

'He's a respectable lecturer.'

'And me?'

'A bit strict. I never knew what to expect in your exams. But you're kind and conscientious.'

'I never thought you were that straightforward. You always seem reserved and silent. I never know what you're thinking.'

'What I'm thinking?'

'What are you thinking of?'

'Of my family.'

'You love your family?'

'They're all I've got.'

'I don't have a family any more. My parents died and I know nothing about my brother and sister.'

'Did they emigrate?'

'No.'

'Did you fall out?'

'No. What I mean is, we each have our own lives. None of us cares about the other.'

For a while there was silence. He looked at her for the first time. Their eyes met. His were unfathomable. Hers were unblinking. He looked at his watch. 'It's one o'clock.'

Desperately she asked, 'How many papers are left? I have fifty. You?'

Looking at the papers, he said, 'About forty.'

He fell silent for a while, and then – 'May I make a call on my mobile?'

He produced his phone and started calling a number. Meanwhile she gazed at him, scrutinizing him.

'Hello, love. How are you, Hajja? ... Maybe another hour ... OK love, take care ... May God protect you.'

Her eyes rounded in amazement. 'Were you talking to your mother?'

He raised his arms and stretched his back, sitting up straight in the chair. 'Yes,' he answered spontaneously.

'Would you like some tea?'

'If you don't have any sugar, then I'd rather not.'

She glanced at him. For the first time she felt he was at ease with her. She didn't like it. Yes, she wanted him to share her bed – but she did not want him to take liberties with her.

She went back to grading, and silence fell for another hour. Finally, he got up with a smile. 'Finished. All the exams have been marked.'

He got up. Yes. Without so much as a word ... and it was all over: all her plans, her hopes. She would remain a virgin forever. She would die a virgin.

In horror she said, 'Don't go, Khaled.'

He looked at her in amazement. Quickly she explained, 'I have something I want to give you.'

He did not understand what she wanted. What in the world had happened to Professor Hanaa?

He remained standing there. She ran to the old kitchen and looked up at the high ceiling. How high it was! How gloomy! And the maid hadn't cleaned it. No, she hadn't cleaned it. When she got back from America, she would have a word with the maid who hadn't cleaned the ceiling. For now she had to seduce the young man who she had begun to hate. Her patience was running out.

She knew what she wanted and what to do. She had planned her scheme carefully.

She flicked the main fuse and the flat went dark, according to plan.

She heaved a sigh of relief. In the dark, she could give him what she wanted. In the dark flat, in the dark of night, maybe he would become intoxicated.

'There's a power cut. I'll bring a candle,' she called out.

A candle was ready at hand.

Lighting it, she went back to the hall. He was holding the flat door open.

'Why are you standing there? Do come in.'

Firmly he said, 'I must go back home.'

Before he could move she once again said, 'Wait five minutes, please; there's a big problem.'

For the first time he looked into her eyes with a hint of doubt, as if he didn't know her.

Curious, he asked, 'A problem?'

Closing the door, placing herself squarely in front of him, she said, feigning distress, 'The house is haunted!'

He burst out laughing. 'Haunted?'

She took his hand firmly before he could move, chattering away so he had no chance to speak, and she dragged him towards the couch. He seemed to have surrendered to her.

'No, listen, Khaled! I've seen them. They come out when there is a power cut. The female floats around like a puff of smoke. Then the male blows out the candle and then relights. And the noises – no one hears them but me.'

Speechless, he looked at her astonished. He sat on the couch silently listening to her.

She was talking rubbish, and she knew it. She did not believe in such things – but she was sure he did. The religious among the lower classes always mix religion with superstition. She had observed this before, in her mother's servant, in the doorman and his wife and so many others.

In a voice filled with fear she said, 'Do you hear something?'

The scene was beginning to tickle his fancy. 'Professor Hanaa, are you joking?'

'Not at all. Don't you believe in *djinn*?'

'Of course I do.'

'Do you know anyone who is possessed?'

'Possessed how?'

'Possessed by a *djinn*.'

'Yes, of course. My aunt was.'

'What did you do about it?'

'I prayed and a pious sheikh helped her. She was very unwell. Imagine – the *djinn* nipped her toe and it was paralysed!'

She sighed in relief, certain that she was approaching her target.

'Khaled, can you hear? What can I do about these noises that are following me around? The day my mother died I heard them all night long and—'

She went quiet. She was not lying any more.

'I was scared of going into her room. I still am. I always feel her standing there next to the bed, scolding me because I'm still alone.'

Was there bitterness in her voice? Could he hear it?

Silence prevailed. They were sitting on the couch. She did not move. She just stared at the candle, and her eyes became spellbound by it. The tears silently flowed over.

This was her chance. She knew that weakness in a woman was a virtue. The problem was she had never ever been weak. No man had ever dared conquer her. Men want to be victorious, want women to be defeated. She hated weakness and defeat.

Wiping away her tears, she said hurriedly, 'I fear the dark. I fear the loneliness and death that surround me.'

He swallowed and started to get up. She caught his hand, saying, 'Don't leave me. Not now. Don't leave me in the dark.'

He sat quietly down again.

She had to act quickly.

Slowly, she put her head on his chest. She started caressing his chest, pressed her body to his and whispered, 'Do you think there are *djinn* in the house?'

Her fingers unbuttoned two buttons of his shirt. She pressed her hand to his chest, felt the strong muscles against her palm. For the first time she felt the rough hair of a man's body. He smelled of pure Egyptian sandalwood soap. Confused, he whispered, 'I don't know.'

He did not move. He did not push her away. What was going on in his head? She would love to know. Maybe she would never know. At the moment she did not care. She did not even care what she felt. There was a mission to be accomplished.

Spontaneously she rubbed her cheek to his neck, whispering, 'I hate darkness and loneliness and silence. And you? Why aren't you speaking?'

He stared at the candle. 'Professor Hanaa – the candle is almost burnt out. Do you want—?'

'I want to give you something. Remember?'

'I don't know if I'm worthy of it.'

'It's not precious any more. It's old and worn.'

'I don't think you possess anything old and worn.'

'Give me a chance.'

'Why me?'

'Don't ask. Don't speak.'

The candle had burnt down. This was her chance. In the darkness, there are no restrictions, no inhibitions. She ran her hands along his body and he held her tight.

She did not like kisses. She didn't know them, she didn't want them. She wanted only one thing. She needed no words any more. All she could feel was her fragile wrist throbbing between his hands. The target was close ...

Clumsily she unzipped his trousers; she moved to his lap and lifted her skirt, and there it was. The end of her virginity. No kisses, no caressing, no passion – he was inside her, and there was relief mixed with a slight pain that did not bother her. The target was achieved.

How much time had passed? She sighed as she smiled inwardly, and lay on the couch, every inch of her body relaxed. He had gone. It was her habit to achieve her goals quickly and skilfully. She had not even removed all her clothes. She hadn't wanted all the niceties now. She had only wanted to carry out the mission.

She had given him the gift. It was five in the morning and she was tired. She had to think about America, the conference and today's glowing success.

***

The call to prayer used to comfort him and give him hope in the coming day. Especially the dawn call to prayer, but today – today!

He closed his eyes, bowed his head and at first did not feel the hand on his shoulder until he heard his friend's voice.

'Khaled. Khaled! It's prayer time. What's wrong with you?'

He did not look at him. It was Muhammad, his blind friend. His closest friend, who was closer to him than his own brother.

Muhammad tapped him on the shoulder again, fumbling his way through the darkness that had been his lot since childhood. He was trying to find his way to his friend, but he couldn't.

'What's wrong with you?' he asked. 'Why are you so late?'

He breathed slowly, as though trying to understand what had taken place the day before. He then calmly said, 'I was helping Professor Hanaa mark exams.'

Feeling for the chair so he could sit, Muhammad smiled. His fingers were used to feeling everything and anything without shame or hesitance.

'The complex Professor Hanaa! Do you remember her lectures? She always explained profusely then gave us a challenging look like we were creatures from another planet and wouldn't understand a word she said. A strong woman, but also a wretched one!'

'Wretched?' he asked rather indifferently. 'Why?'

'I don't know. At her age – how old is she? Late thirties I would say.'

Muhammad was quiet for a moment then chirped up as an idea struck him. 'Do you think she's still a virgin?'

Khaled answered in annoyance. 'It's *harām* to speak of women's honour during the dawn prayers. Go and pray.'

'And you? Why aren't you going to pray? What have you done? Have you been with a prostitute?'

Angrily he burst out, 'How could you say such a thing?'

'I was joking! You're never laid-back about dawn prayers. Why today?'

He did not utter a word. He felt uncommonly upset.

Slyly Muhammad said, 'Honestly, haven't you wondered if she is a virgin? I think she is. Her voice has a strange note of melancholy. Is she beautiful?'

'I don't know. Maybe.'

'You used to describe everything to me.'

'Are we going to talk about her all night? I'm tired.'

'Let's talk about Safaa then. How I yearn for a woman and you could marry Safaa in an instant and yet you don't!'

'Perhaps I will.'

'Have you decided to go back to her? That would be for the best. She's a nice girl and she loves you. Your mother and your sister don't want you to get married but you need to be married. We all need marriage. Especially men. It's different for women. A woman doesn't have the same needs we do. She can live without a husband. She can remain a virgin if she wants; a man can't.'

'True, if she wants.'

'So, she's a virgin?'

He pondered for a while. 'Either she is one or she was one.'

'I don't understand.'

'It doesn't matter. Go pray.'

'What's up, Khaled?'

'Today my life was turned upside down. Something I neither wanted nor expected has become a burden on my shoulders. May God forgive me! I didn't want it. Go and pray! Pray for me and never ask me what happened today!'

Chapter 2

Carrying the exam papers, Professor Hanaa made her way towards her old Peugeot while the doorman looked on in contempt. Turning away he said, 'God preserve us!'

She stopped in her stride, turned around in terror and burst at him, 'Why are you saying that?'

He shifted his eyes away from her, mumbling something she could not hear. She knew why he was saying what he had said and she did not know what to do. Berate him? Threaten him? Bribe him? Justify herself to him? Defend herself?

She told herself that if she needed to explain herself to the doorman every day in this country, just because she was a woman, then it would be better if she went somewhere more civilized. It never crossed her mind to give the doorman ten pounds and explain that Khaled was her student. Ten pounds would have been sufficient to open the closed doors in his brain! Ten pounds would have been enough to make him feel like the private bodyguard of a French princess – if there was such a thing as a French princess! Ten pounds would have been enough to open up his heart, purge his conscience and explain the situation. She, however, was not planning to sacrifice ten pounds. She had no intention of starting to pay bribes now.

For the first time in her life, she felt completely free. A load had been lifted from her shoulders and the pain and shame she had felt had vanished. She would travel to the conference, she would (or she would not) meet Ramy in America ... in any case, she was no longer a virgin. Now she had to concentrate on the conference.

As she was driving to the airport, the image of her flat kept lingering in her mind. She loved it beyond all imagination. The flat had not changed much since her mother's death. She kept everything as it had been, and preserved all the furniture and all that was of value. She had no children to wear it out, nor visitors who would spoil the upholstery on her living room couch. The sixties-style, ornately gilt living room furniture had been bought by her mother when she got married, and was always covered in plain, clean, white dust covers. The video player she had bought a decade ago was also clean and covered with a crochet cover she had got years before when at a conference in Germany. Even the remote control for the video was in mint condition, still covered in cellophane, just like the television, for which she had a special cover. She covered it every night before going to bed, since the pollution in Cairo was unlike anywhere else in the world. She was very fond of her things; they were all she had.

The large hall in her flat contained next to no furniture, but to its left lay the dining room, the most beautiful area in the house; it was her pride and joy with its old brown table made of arrowwood and its tall, grand cabinet with shelves of glass.

The cabinet enclosed all her possessions – her life. Like her father, she loved antiques and bought many of them. If there was anything she splurged her money on, it was vases, statuettes and old silver cutlery sets. Her fortune rested in this immense cabinet, the contents of which stood proudly but wearily, waiting for someone to spare them a second glance.

The long, narrow corridor, as long as life itself, was generally dark, as she was saving electricity. Her parents' bedroom, which was now hers, lay at the end of the corridor. Next to it were two rooms she never entered; one had been her brother's, and the other one she used to share with her sister. Then there was the old bathroom filled with scented air freshener and all kinds of therapeutic oils, like lavender and camomile, to calm the nerves while bathing.

This was Professor Hanaa's home. She had bought out her siblings' shares in the inheritance, so as to have it all to herself, to relive her memories, to remember her mother and father and to hear their voices with the sound of music every morning. She liked this way of life. But sometimes ... sometimes the long nights with thick clouds enveloped her cold body and aroused her without quenching her thirst for rest, strangling her without ever killing her. She feared those nights. God help whoever met her the next morning; they were greeted by a violent outburst, fuelled by her pent-up, inexhaustible energy.

Now, before reaching the airport, she felt a need to pass through Boulaq. She wanted to see Boulaq before she travelled: just out of curiosity, nothing more. She had passed by it every now and then but had never regarded the district as being of any significance to her life – it was just a lower-class area with little beauty and too many people. Boulaq for her was foul smells, grey old buildings smeared with dust, pollution and donkey droppings, and children playing on the street with no sense of their surroundings nor of the dirt. In Boulaq green is not a word found in dictionaries.

The only thing that she ever noticed was the droves of people who flocked to the ful and falafel shops in the morning and how they seemed glued to each other. So many people, such an incredible mass of humanity that moved systematically and monotonously in unnerving silence and suppressed screams.

The loud music that blasted from the shops caught her attention. Each shop in Boulaq had a different song playing, and they all blended together into one huge cacophony. All stuffed together exactly like the people!

***

She rested her head against the aeroplane seat. The stream of air from the air conditioning was aimed straight at her right eye. Travelling makes the imagination immune and the memories fresh. Memories were dripping from her mind. She shut her eyes and started conjuring up images from her past, from twenty years ago. Images of a girl who was silently in love with her colleague. Ramy was quiet, shy and hesitant. She liked his meekness and indecisiveness. They had both taken appointments at the department. They grew close – they would talk about Shakespeare and Dickens for hours on end. He was wise and mature and would contemplate the world and the universe. A year passed, while she remained his colleague and remained silently in love with him. He wanted to emigrate to America. He wanted to go there on an academic travel grant. She won the grant.

She wanted to know how he felt towards her. He was forever talking about his mother and how he respected her: what his mother wanted; what she expected; never about herself and him. She remembered the decisive day of their relationship, just before she travelled to the US. She sat before him in the office as she usually did. Their desks were opposite each other. This time she left her chair and rested her arm on his desk. Nervously, she fiddled with the papers and rubbed her fingers. In despair, she asked, 'Dare I dream?'

Ramy swallowed, bowed his head and hoarsely whispered, 'No.'

She was not used to taking no for an answer. She was strong, she took the initiative. She was perceptive enough to know his feelings towards her, and she wanted to offer him a helping hand. She loved a challenge. A victory. Although his answer disappointed her, perhaps she had expected it from the beginning. She challenged him again, once more probing him and pushing him to declare his love. 'Was I mistaken? Was it all just my imagination? Was I that stupid?'

'You are not stupid, Hanaa,' he said with great feeling.

Angrily she said, 'I am leaving Egypt in a week's time.'

Looking down at the floor, he said, 'I know. Hanaa ... I ... didn't dare dream but I—'

He fell silent for a while then, 'What's the use? Even if I did share your feelings, what's the use? You know, don't you?'

Triumphantly she cried, 'You do feel the same way about me.'

He smiled, saying in a mixture of exasperation and fear, 'You yourself are a problem. You ... are like a massive lorry … no one can control you ... Do you know that?'

'Me? A lorry!?' she exclaimed angrily.

'Don't corner me, Hanaa. Forget ... forgetting is one of God's most wonderful blessings.'

She opened her eyes, his words ringing in her ears. 'Forget ... forget.'

She might never see Ramy again. Why had she thought she would?

Anyway, who was Ramy now? Was he the same young man she had loved twenty years ago? She recalled her days in America: her loneliness, her perseverance, her patience, her determination and her dream of him day after day. He might have said she should not dare dream. But she dared do everything! If only now he knew that she dared do everything. When it was Ramy's turn to leave on a grant, he never returned from America.

He settled there, married an Egyptian, and no one ever heard anything of him again.

She sighed wearily, exhausted after the long day she had yesterday. Ramy came from a family very similar to her own. He came from Mohandeseen District and spoke to her with awe and respect. He was not from Boulaq. He did not feel his way through the shells of people who were crushed a thousand times a day. Would she see Ramy? And if she did see him, how would she tell him she was no longer a virgin? How?!

Would she ever stop thinking of him? Had he not been out of her life for years?

There was this urge inside her to show him that she was now a woman, to openly declare the end of her spinsterhood.

She did not like going to America. She remembered only the days of loneliness, work and despair. She looked for him in every face at the conference, but to no avail. She gave a lecture on Victorian women's literature, then went and sat in the vast hall of the University of California, drinking healthy sugar-free juice and contemplating her life.

What would she do, now that she had lost her virginity?

She listened to the English surrounding her, her eyes seeing nothing but a single floor-tile, a white marble tile with some small grooves. What was she to do about Khaled?

Nothing. He was simply a means to an end and she had attained the end she wanted. Now, there was no need for the means.

Had she made a bad choice? No. Khaled was a simple, kind person; he was pious and dependable. He would not say a word. If he did, she would strangle him with her bare hands. He needed to know that. She would have to make it clear to him when she returned.

There was a small groove in the tile. Had it been there long or was it new?

She would make it plain that if he uttered a word she would …

Those shoes that American woman was wearing, with those incredibly high heels, how could she walk in them? She walked with her legs far apart like a dinosaur, as though she could not walk properly yet.

If he so much as uttered a word!

She heard a voice she knew. She looked up from the ground expecting to see him. Ramy. Had she not come here for Ramy? This was his university. She had to see Ramy.

* * *

During the coffee break at the conference, she saw a man. The room was full. There were so many different English accents. Some bothered her, while others were more pleasant to listen to.

But it was not Ramy she saw. It was a man she did not know. In his features, she saw the passage of time, and was afraid of how she might appear to him.

He sat down at the table next to her, a man in his forties. His hair was mostly grey. His features had changed: his cheeks were chubbier, wrinkles were settling around his eyes and his double chin bore witness to a hard and yet rich life. The look in his eyes had changed: it was more broken, more cold. He was another man.

His voice had not changed, however. If only he would speak.

'Ramy!' she cried eagerly, her heart pounding.

His smile was both hesitant and annoyed. 'Hanaa. How are you? No, I won't ask. You're fine, of course. Have you been made head of department yet?'

She had expected a different question, one he did not ask: How many children have you got? What is your husband's name? Are you still a virgin?

'No, I haven't been made head yet,' she said, staring at his pudgy fingers that were alien to her and at the wedding band that he had rammed on to one of them and forgotten forever.

'But you still read and work a lot. I read your latest paper.'

She scrutinized his face, unsure if it was jealousy or admiration which she saw there.

He did not ask her. Why?

Looking at her with a hint of gentleness, he sighed, 'How are you, Hanaa? It's been a lifetime since I last saw you. What's life been doing to you?

Challengingly she asked, 'What's life been doing to you?'

'A lot.'

He fell silent for a second, then: 'Did you come here to see me?'

She panicked.

She opened her mouth to speak but he hastily interrupted, 'Of course you came to see me. I was off yesterday. That's why I didn't attend your lecture. I'm sorry. I knew one day you'd come and when you did, you'd criticize my research, challenge my conclusions and you'd be the triumphant one.'

Proudly she said, 'I definitely publish more than you do.'

He whispered warmly, 'And you are better looking than me! Exactly like you were twenty years ago. Of course you never got married.'

'What makes you say that?'

'Because I know there isn't a man in the world who could dominate you.'

'Maybe I married a foreigner.'

'I said no man *in the world*, not in Egypt. Wow, Hanaa! It's been a lifetime!'

'Are you happy that you stayed in the US?'

After a moment's silence, he said, 'What's the difference between America and Egypt?'

'Democracy, freedom, justice!'

He smiled scornfully. 'There is neither justice nor democracy in any country in the world. The powerful lay down the law, the weak follow it. But when will you become head of the department?'

'When Samy and the likes of him drop dead!'

'Samy Fathy! He's head of the department?! You really are unlucky!'

She opened her mouth. How was she to tell him she had lost her virginity? Could she tell him?

What an idiot she was. She had prepared everything for this day and now, she did not know how to tell him!

Once again she asked, 'Are you coming back to Egypt soon?'

'No,' he immediately answered.

'Your wife likes America?'

'She hates it as much as she hates my mother, but she lives in America with my mother. Poor thing. Well actually, I'm the poor thing. I have to put up with America and my wife and my mother!'

She smiled. At least he did not seem happy. At least he didn't have everything while she had nothing.

There was a moment of silence. An awkward moment. Then he glanced at his watch and she jumped up saying, 'I'm leaving tomorrow.'

Rather embarrassed he said, 'I can't invite you to my place – my wife is away. I too am leaving tomorrow.'

Smiling coldly she replied, 'It's not important, Ramy. Next time.'

'Oh yes, next time,' he said eagerly.

'By the way,' she said with a sly smile, 'you don't know everything about me, although you think you do.'

He looked at her for a few seconds not understanding what she meant.

'I have not claimed that I do,' he said.

Once more she smiled triumphantly, ignoring his reply. 'God willing, I'll see you again soon.'

He nodded in agreement, still trying and failing to understand her last comment. Maybe he would not think about her much. The trip to America had been short and confusing.

'Dare I dream?' she asked.

'No!'

She smiled sarcastically. She was naive and strong, uncomfortable in the presence of any male other than Ramy. She hated loud voices, domination and oppression.

And even though her father had been a calm, rational man, she saw the suppression of women all around her.

She often felt male arms to be dominating and smothering, the male voice threatening and terrifying. She saw male oppression all around her. She hated the Egyptian male, with his violence and autocracy.

Sometimes, she pictured herself alone in a chair in a dark room. Then a man would lean over to scare her, threaten her, trap her between the arms of the chair and proceed to torture her. This would not happen – she would not allow it – but she imagined it, and imagining was sufficient to make her reject anyone who proposed marriage to her if their voice was too loud, if they laughed too much or if they did not talk to her about her research and her future.

Her imagination conjured up this image, framed in gold, and hung on the wall of her mind: the image of a man leaning over, trapping her in her chair and dictating his rules – threatening, terrifying and stifling her.

Her brother was of the annoying kind: he had been her mother's favourite, she her father's. Because she was the youngest, she had not suffered too much at the hands of her brother. Her sister Leila, however, had often been terrorized by him, and Hanaa had often been witness to this physical and mental abuse.

To her students, Professor Hanaa always said, 'The men in this country need some surgery to remove all the excesses, the backward ideas, the bad upbringing and ... and ...'

No one agreed with her: neither her male students nor her female ones.

She returned to Egypt. Now she had to face Khaled again.

If he uttered a word, she would behead him quietly and skilfully with a sharp knife. The trip had been a success; as she had expected, her lecture had gone down well. She had found Ramy and met with him: that was the best thing about the whole trip. He knew now that she was more successful than he was, that she was happy, that she was not crying after him while he had founded a family. He knew now that she might not be a virgin. Yes, he had to know. He used to understand her so well in the past. Now she could make a fresh start, and the first thing she would do would be to confront Dr Samy, her department head, and defeat him!

She arrived back at her flat in the dead of night. She was exhausted. She unlocked the door, walked in and realized that everything was soaked in water. She had inadvertently left the plug stopping the plug hole in the bathroom sink, and water was now overflowing from a leaking tap. A water leak was the last thing she needed!

Her legs barely supporting her, she called the doorman.

For hours she sat in the hallway, waiting for the plumber.

She gazed at the total destruction of her flat.

Anticipating her answer, the doorman cautiously said, 'The plumber wants three hundred pounds.'

She glared at him disdainfully. 'Why! Has he put in a new bathroom? Do you think I'm made of money?'

He knew Professor Hanaa well; he knew how penny-pinching she was; he felt sorry for the plumber.

The plumber finished changing the bathroom tap.

She heaved a sigh of relief and went into the bathroom like a primary school inspector. She looked at the tap in agitation; this was a different tap.

The man looked at her as if she were talking Greek. 'Of course,' he said. 'I told you I was going to change it.'

With great determination she said, 'This tap is silver with a gold stripe. Mine was silver with a white stripe! This is a different tap!'

'I didn't find one exactly the same as yours,' he said impatiently.

'And I want a tap exactly like mine. I will not accept this tap,' she said firmly.

Annoyed the plumber snapped, 'Madam Hanaa! I have other work to do. Give me my money so I can get going!'

'I want a tap like mine,' she said adamantly, 'I will not give you a penny for this one.'

Frustrated he shouted, 'Dear God, grant me patience! I said there wasn't one like yours!'

She looked at him furiously. 'You won't get a penny if you don't change this tap. And I am not Madam Hanaa; I am Professor Hanaa! Don't you dare talk to me like that. Go on, get out of my house!'

The man mumbled something then left, saying, 'God have mercy on me.'

She locked the door behind him in disgust then opened all the windows, washed her hands and prepared for bed. She would think about the tap tomorrow. Tomorrow she would return to the university.

She knew he would come. Of course he would come. Perhaps he would propose marriage out of a sense of guilt. Maybe he would try to use her to promote himself. Maybe he would come to tell her off! She knew that night would not just pass as she wished it to, as something that was over and done with. There had to be consequences. She felt no remorse. No remorse at all.

She smiled at him, seeing him in a new light after what had happened.

'Khaled, how are you? I knew you'd come,' she said.

He looked at her, professing astonishment. 'Was the reason for what happened between us that I came to see you? It's not every day that a girl loses her virginity just to see a man – or at least I hope that is not how it is with all women. If you wanted me to come to your office, professor, you only needed to say so and nothing else.'

'You talk about me as if I were an ordinary Egyptian woman and you know very well I'm not.'

He raised his eyebrows in an expression of astonishment and sarcasm. 'No? You aren't Egyptian? Then where are you from?'

'Khaled. You wouldn't understand.'

'Yes, you're right. I won't understand.'

'Are you here to ask me to marry you?'

Indifferently he replied, 'Perhaps. I came to understand. If there is anything to be understood. Professor Hanaa, all I know about you is that your house is haunted and you are scared of the dark. And you know nothing about me except that my aunt was possessed. Is there anything more I could know about a woman who gave herself to me without kissing me once?'

She looked at him aghast. 'Please don't talk to me like that.'

In a tone of sarcasm mixed with seriousness he said, 'I'm just wondering. I apologize of course – I should act in a way that is worthy of you.'

'How?'

'By making love to you the way I dreamt of.'

'You dreamt of me?'

'Not of you in particular, but of the first time I had a woman.'

'It was your first time?'

'Yes, I think so. Sort of the first time I really made love to a woman. I'm God-fearing, you know.'

She fell silent for a while. Then she asked, 'You are a God-fearing, Middle Eastern, Egyptian man and you have dreams and expectations. What do you dream of? What do you expect from a woman?'

She surprised him with her question, with her strange words: 'Egyptian', 'Middle Eastern', 'God-fearing' – as if he belonged to another world, one she didn't know.

Calmly he replied, 'What do I expect from a woman? As a Middle Eastern man? I expect her to obey me throughout the day, and I obey her at night. I expect her to be made up and dressed in silk and to fill the house with the scent of incense. I expect her to cook a whole sheep for me every day; to adore me and look at me in fear and submissiveness; to await me while I make my choice between her and my other wives and to be ecstatic if I choose her; to pay me the due obedience and allegiance; and to await her turn every week in suspense and fear that she may not please me, so that I scorn her and choose another—'

'Wait a minute. You're making fun of me, aren't you? I asked you a question. Why can't you just answer it? What do you expect of a woman – your woman?'

He leaned back in the chair. 'Not much; I don't expect much. Just what every man expects.'

'What does every man expect? What do you expect?'

'I want a woman who understands me, who backs me, stands by me and supports me. I want her to be intelligent, educated, cultured, calm, obedient and loving. I don't want a woman who quarrels with me the whole time and challenges me daily. You see, professor, a man in this country is like a camel in the desert suffering from thirst, hunger and a heavy load. And yet he cannot stop, he must march on despite the exhaustion brought about by the path and the heat, by humiliation and degradation. He wants to come home to a warm loving woman, not one who will smother him, control him or think herself better than him. Do you get what I mean, Professor Hanaa?'

'You're too kind, Khaled. You really aren't asking for much. Let's see what you said; maybe we can make use of it. You want her calm and obedient. Maybe you should buy a cat. No wait, cats aren't obedient! A cow. You should buy a cow. Cows are obedient.'

'You seem to like the first description I gave of the woman I want and not the second. Never mind. Professor Hanaa, I have a final question before I go. Why? Why now? And do you expect something of me?'

Sternly she said, 'Yes, of course. I expect you not to speak of this, with me or with anyone else. I trust you, Khaled, but I don't understand you and I don't like the sarcastic tone you take with me.'

'Well pardon me, professor, but I need to make sure I understand what you mean. You want me to forget I made love to you and was the first man in your life, that you caused me to sin and turned my life upside down?'

'I'm the one who should be complaining, not you.'

'And why aren't you? Why don't you demand marriage? It doesn't matter. I understand, professor.'

'If you breathe a word, I'll kill you. I'll kill you with my bare hands!' she hissed.

He drew nearer and whispered derisively, 'I know you're capable of it. Thanks for seeing me. Goodbye, professor.'

* * *

Everyone steals; everyone sucks up to those in power and turns a blind eye to transgressions. However, there are thieves who have finesse and there are crude ones; and crudity is despised by all Egyptians. It was, therefore, perfectly normal for Professor Samy to accept a few gifts, invitations and services.

The fact that Professor Samy's son got a distinction for his master's degree in philosophy was also perfectly normal, just as his plagiarizing an earlier master's thesis from another university was normal and acceptable.

However, the fact that Professor Samy's son plagiarized the thesis of a person who was alive and well, and teaching at a regional university – that, of course, showed lack of finesse.

Everything was acceptable except lack of finesse.

To steal with finesse was permissible, but bold-faced crude stealing was definitely not. Things apparently had become a bit confused for Professor Samy. He had begun to forget the ropes of his job. He had become impolite, crude and bold. Very, very bold.

The Dean was getting fed up with his scandals, with his crude manner with those around him and those who asked for his help. He was not above demanding a Mercedes for a student to pass in his subject or some service in return for a grant. He demanded boldly with no sense of guilt, without first testing the waters and making sure of the reception.

A gift was given, not demanded! He never understood that.

The Dean was getting seriously annoyed, particularly after Professor Samy bought the new Mercedes following the scandal of his son, the holder of a master's degree with distinction.

The university needed fresh blood, a presentable front ... a woman. Yes. It needed a woman. A woman in the position of department head was the greatest proof that Egypt was a progressive country that did not discriminate between men and women when it came to filling positions.

The choice lay between two women, Maysah and Hanaa, and they were poles apart.

Maysah was in her early fifties, married, with three children. She wore a headscarf, her husband was a professor at the Faculty of Medicine and the students loved her. Hanaa was reclusive and difficult. She was known for her motto: 'equality in injustice'. She was fair, produced many papers and had made a name for herself abroad.

The Dean had not decided yet. He had to meet with both Maysah and Hanaa.

The time came for his interview with Hanaa. She fixed her sharp eyes on him in a way he did not like. He did not know if he was capable of dealing with her. Professor Maysah, on the other hand, was cheerful. She talked about her children all the time and was a shining example of an Egyptian woman. Should she one day decide to accept a bribe, or turn a blind eye to a grievance, or extend some service to a relative, she would do it with finesse and grace, without crudity.

The choice seemed straightforward and easy, and the university as an institution needed to be reinvigorated.

But then, Professor Hanaa was loyal – and her allegiance would be to the institution itself, not to an individual.

To the government!

Who in this day and age was loyal to the government? In Egypt, whoever gave their allegiance to the government was a traitor to land and country, worthy of being stoned, of having stale bread and American flour hurled at them!

And yet Hanaa's allegiance was to the Establishment!

He had never met anyone quite like Professor Hanaa before. She still owed her allegiance to the university, not to her parents, her sister, her relatives, the neighbours, her brothers in Islam, her brothers in Christianity, nor her fellow countrymen!

Her allegiance was to the Establishment!

He had to think about Maysah and Hanaa again. He asked Hanaa to go on a trip with the Students' Union, along with a number of lecturers and professors. He wanted to hear everyone's reaction.

Although she sensed the Dean's sudden interest in her and his sudden hatred for Samy, Hanaa did not quite know what was going on in his head. If the Dean wanted her to go on the Students' Union trip, then she had to do what he wanted. In fact it was a happy day if the Dean remembered her enough to ask her for something – anything. She remembered her private school and the teacher she had liked because she was calm and hard-working. She always delegated the honourable tasks, like carrying the copybooks from one class to another, wiping the board or going to get chalk. Hanaa thought her schooldays would never end, that the school was still there – different-looking but there – and she was being given an honourable task and should feel grateful for having been singled out.

Her black hair was pulled back in a ponytail as usual. She wore a bright printed dress and high-heeled black shoes. She looked as if she had just walked out of a soap advert from the nineteen fifties.

This time, however, she took a bit more care with her appearance than usual, and applied a little eyeliner as well as some pink lipstick.

She wanted the trip to pass smoothly, to spend the time reading as usual, to forget the heat of Cairo and sit beneath a tall palm tree quietly contemplating the universe without being disturbed. Her problem was that she got bored with people too quickly.

Salma the lecturer's farm was bigger than the entire district of Shubra – and of course less densely populated.

Salma was looking proudly around and asking them all if they needed anything.

Professor Hanaa avoided looking at Khaled: she ignored him. She found a tree, brought out the rug she had prepared the day before yesterday, placed it beneath her and sat down. Out of her bag she brought a flask of hot water and a washed and carefully dried cup. She began to drink the hot water the way she did every morning – with no tea or coffee, just water to purge her stomach. She usually did not take breakfast.

She brought out her beloved anthology of Elizabethan poetry and started reading intently.

Suddenly, the sound of loud music penetrated her ears:

My life, your swaying figure
aroused feelings within me.
You're the most beautiful person to me.
Sublime is the one who created you.

Without looking around she quietly said, 'The music is too loud.'

She heard a girl whisper, 'Sorry, professor.'

She turned around and stared at the girl next to her ... at her eyes. She had seen them before. She was young, no more than eighteen, wearing a blue veil, colourful clothes, eyeliner, blusher and gold jewellery.

The girl smiled. Drawing nearer, she said, 'You see, I love Abdel Halim very much, and Khaled does too. Especially this song. He loves it so much.'

Scrutinizing the girl, Hanaa quipped, 'Are you his sister?'

Laughing heartily she said, 'Yes.'

The girl was neither shy nor apprehensive, and Hanaa realized she was not yet at university.

She could hear voices all around her. She gazed at the large garden and the football pitch that the students had immediately improvised. He was playing ball so skilfully, as though he had spent his childhood practising in the narrow streets of Boulaq. Of course that was what his childhood had been like. She, on the other hand, had spent her childhood trying to learn to play the piano, listening to classical music with her father, visiting her aunts ... all in all, acting like a successful girl from a well-to-do family.

Her eyes followed him as he ran across the field, full of vigour and abandonment, calling out forcefully to the other players. She fixed her eyes on him, on his youthful body. She kept trying to visualize him as a student. She could not. Maybe she would never again be able to.

He was bursting with vitality, his sweat was pouring down and the veins of his neck seemed to be screaming with him as he defiantly demanded the ball.

She smiled scornfully at herself and at the adolescent feelings she was experiencing.

She averted her eyes and began to read once more, until the girl approached her and whispered, 'You're Professor Hanaa, aren't you?'

'Yes,' she replied without looking up.

Sitting down on Professor Hanaa's rug, the girl burst out, 'I really want to join the English department. I'm in the last year of secondary school. Khaled says he'll help me.'

She sensed danger approaching and frowned in annoyance, her blood pressure rising.

How could she get rid of the girl? It wasn't really her words that upset Hanaa. It was the girl sitting close to her like that. And on her rug! She would have to wash it a few times. Moreover, it was only a small rug, just big enough for one person.

'Er ...' she muttered.

'Shaimaa,' the girl said quickly.

'Shaimaa, could you—'

Shaimaa interrupted her in the tone of someone about to reveal a great secret. 'You see that girl over there talking to Muhammad under the tree? That's Safaa, the girl Khaled was in love with.'

The subject interested her all of a sudden. She grabbed the part of the rug next to the girl's leg and, pulling it, enquired, 'And why didn't he marry her?'

'Because Mum doesn't like her!' Shaimaa burst out. 'Safaa didn't like us either. She wanted to take him away from us ... and she's greedy and there's something about her not quite right. I mean, she doesn't love him. It's just pretence.'

She began to tug firmly at the rug – but to no avail.

'Professor Hanaa, is there something wrong?'

'There was something on the rug. Would you get up for a minute?'

Shaimaa stood up and Hanaa snatched away the rug from beneath her, much relieved. 'That's better,' she said.

Shaimaa stared in astonishment, but Hanaa did not attempt to explain. She sat down, and – finding the conversation extremely interesting – asked abruptly, 'And he left her because you and your mother didn't like her?'

'Yes, of course – and for other reasons as well. Khaled is the man of the family now. He has responsibilities.'

'Does he beat you?'

'Huh?'

'Does your brother beat you?'

'Sometimes. But not like my friend Sameeha – her brother beats her indiscriminately,' she answered indifferently. She did not seem in the least embarrassed, as if a beating was a brother's undisputed right.

'Why does he beat you?' Hanaa asked, looking annoyed.

She sensed Shaimaa's sudden uneasiness with the conversation. In an instant, Shaimaa remembered the violent row she had had with her brother five months ago, when she had been late because she had stayed on at her friend's house till midnight. That day ... her friend had a gorgeous brother and Shaimaa loved to talk – just talk – with Mr Gorgeous. She got so caught up in talking that she lost track of time. When she got home, Khaled was in the worst state she had seen him in since his father's death. She both feared and taunted him. When he asked her why she had been late, she answered boldly, 'Are you my father? You? My father is dead! You are merely my brother! Just because you provide for me doesn't mean you can tell me what to do.'

Her mother had overheard the exchange, her mouth gaping as if her daughter had just announced that she was three months pregnant by a stranger. And Shaimaa was a good girl; she would never be three months pregnant! All that had taken place was talk and a few furtive caresses ... for which, of course, she should not be taxed so harshly! Was there a girl in the whole of Egypt who had not done that? Perhaps her friend, the gorgeous boy's sister, had not done it yet, but there was a time for everything.

That day, her brother had slapped her in the face. He had been cruel, he was like a lion marking its territory, and he marked it all right! She had not been late since. What really got on her nerves was the way her mother had smiled in relief when her brother declared his absolute authority over her: that she was in his care, that he was now her father and that she need only concentrate on her studies, that she should sometimes spare a thought for her mother and brother and all those who worked day and night so she could get an education and go to university. She wanted Mr Gorgeous and wanted to enjoy a little taste of life's pleasures.

Never mind. In spite of everything, her brother was kind. He did not tighten the noose too much. Most of the time he worked away from home. He bought her everything she wanted, asked after her every day and egged her on to succeed. Sometimes she hated the way he pushed and challenged her, his dreams of her rosy future: that she should go on to university, graduate and work and ... and ...

In any case, this professor was indescribably stupid! What kind of question was that to ask?

Was there a brother in Egypt who had not beaten his sister at least once? Maybe not the whole of Egypt. In Boulaq? At school? On her street? Really, educated people sometimes said the strangest things!

This was what was going through her head, but she did not utter a word.

Hanaa was scrutinizing her as if she was reading her mind. She said, 'Tell me about Safaa.'

She burst out excitedly, 'You know, professor, once I was very unwell – I couldn't breathe properly. My mum gave me a glass of water with sugar and some homemade caramel. Safaa was visiting us that day, pretending she liked us. When she saw I was about to faint, she held my hand and said sweet things; all lies. When she held my hand, I felt she wasn't warm, just putting on an act. I felt sorry for my brother – he would be marrying an actress. So I told him at once.'

Hanaa put down her book, for the conversation was of extreme interest to her, especially the bit about holding hands, warmth and feelings.

Her eyes were once more drawn to the pitch. Again she looked at Khaled, just as his blind friend Muhammad approached him cautiously. He was about to fall, but Khaled, without a second's thought, grabbed his arm and started explaining what had been going on in the match up to that point. It was as if he had trained himself to be his friend's eyes. To back and support him.

It was not difficult to see that Khaled relished the role of the saviour, the responsible man!

Once again she picked up her book and started to read. Shaimaa got fed up sitting on the ground. Getting up she said, 'Would you like anything, professor? Can I get you a sandwich or something?'

'No, thank you.'

'Mum made liver sandwiches and date biscuits. Would you like a biscuit then?'

'No thank you,' she said irritably.

She hated the idea of liver with oil and garlic and biscuits full of butter, sugar, dust and filth.

She looked at Safaa, scrutinizing her. She was dark-skinned with a red veil and tight clothes. She was a young woman, no older than twenty, with Egyptian features. She was full-lipped and used this to her advantage by applying a generous amount of lipstick.

Why had Safaa come on this trip? Maybe she wanted to get back with Khaled. Maybe Muhammad had invited her. Maybe she had come to taunt him and show him she did not care.

Her eyes met Safaa's. She smiled, got up carrying the rug and made for Safaa. She sat down next to her, extended her hand and said, 'I'm Professor Hanaa.'

In a mixture of bewilderment and admiration Safaa said, 'Hello, professor ...'

'I'm in the same department as Khaled. And you?'

She swallowed nervously, saying, 'There is nothing between us any more.'

'No?' asked Hanaa eagerly.

'No. Thanks to his mother and his sister. They don't want him ever to get married.'

Her accent and her manner were similar to those of Shaimaa. She had a strange touch of vulgarity that was alien to Hanaa and which she did not detect in Khaled. She over-articulated the 't' sound and her hands and lips played a greater part than her tongue when she spoke. Her aspirated 't' was a clear marker of her lower class.

These manners were strange and unknown to her.

With a hint of pain Safaa said, 'I know he loves me.'

'He loves you?' Hanaa asked, opening her eyes wide and raising her eyebrows. 'How do you know?'

'Oh, I know. But he's stubborn and vain and totally under his mother and sister's thumb.'

Then she whispered in Hanaa's ear, 'They've cast a spell on him.'

She nodded, 'Of course!'

Safaa burst out, 'But he's kind-hearted and he loves me.'

In a tone of command, Hanaa asked, 'And do you love him?'

'Yes. I have loved him my whole life.'

'How old are you?'

'Twenty.'

Hanaa fell silent for a while, then continued in a serious tone, 'Safaa, listen to me. Khaled will never be of any use to you. If he goes on living under his mother and sister's influence, your life will be hell. Don't you ever, ever go back to him. If he wants you, he'll come back to you. If you go back to him, he'll use and abuse you then cast you aside. Do you get it?'

She nodded her head, 'My mother says that too. He also doesn't want me to contradict him. If I ever say no, he gets upset and won't talk to me and says "I'm the man" and that kind of thing.'

Hanaa burst out, 'Don't you dare go back to him. He'll torment you. Listen Safaa – I'm always at the university. If you need anything just come, and I'll get you a much better bridegroom.'

For a moment Hanaa glanced over at Khaled with rage against him and desire for him both burning within her.

He was toying with the ball: approaching it, encircling it, pinning it down, then kicking it up high. It was as if he withdrew, yearned, flirted then approached once more. When another player kicked the ball, he would shout. Agitated sweat streamed down his neck, almost pouring forth and splashing all over the place.

Again he approached and fought, cornering the ball like a fox in anticipation, nervous, confident and with passion – yes, with great passion.

She got up before she lost her composure. Men! How ugly they were in their tyranny and authority and—

How she pitied Safaa! She had to make sure Safaa was all right and that she would never, ever marry Khaled.

The Dean liked the democracy which was enjoyed by everyone. He loved talking to the professors on an individual basis and the exchange of ideas and free discussion. Naturally, he had to intervene immediately whenever a discussion crossed the boundaries of the acceptable, in which case he would bring the professor involved before the disciplinary panel and add a little something to their file in the form of a black mark – for 'troublemaker'. He asked a lot of questions, made a great number of demands and was careful with promotions and the like. He did listen patiently, but as one listens to a television series; then he would do what he wanted, which usually involved attempting to do the opposite of what everyone else wanted, for in the modern system of democracy, doing what others wanted was the first step towards collapse. The Dean had his own philosophy.

Every day we see democratic societies collapsing and countries being divided in the name of democracy.

Why should we trust in humanity in general when we know people are prone to making mistakes, to forgetting and to everything else!

He listened to people's opinions on Professor Hanaa and Professor Maysah. The general consensus was that Professor Maysah was easy to work with; she was like a mother or a sister, a Hajja, a dignified woman whom God loved. As for Hanaa, she was respected but difficult to work with: demanding, weird, complex, a spinster. And she would give the department hell.

So, in the interest of democracy, and for the love of the people and the people's rule, the Dean decided to appoint Professor Hanaa as Head of Department.

Chapter 3

As soon as Hanaa heard of her outstanding victory, of the change in the course of events and of the sovereignty of the law, two people immediately jumped into her mind: Abdel Hamid, Professor Samy's secretary, and Khaled.

Abdel Hamid was 'as lost as an orphan at the villains' banquet', as the saying goes. His fate, now in Hanaa's hands, was gloomy indeed. She only needed a moment to crush him and throw him to the rats for dinner.

Power made her tipsy. It gave her such ecstasy as she had never known before! The past and the present vanished, and Ramy was dwarfed into insignificance, playing no role in the writing of history.

Abdel Hamid ...

How often had he kept her waiting for hours to meet His Excellency, Professor Samy? How often had he answered her with blatant impertinence? As if she were an insect, not a fully qualified professor? Oh, time and again ... and again ... and again!

Now he was her secretary. She would toy with him, like a cat toys with a mouse before it devours it. Or maybe she should crush him – grate him like an old piece of cheese and then leave him for the rats to eat!

Ah! How beautiful was Egypt! Justice! The key to happiness!

At last there was justice. She had thought Egypt was slipping through her fingers, just like her life. Now her life and Egypt were firmly in her hands. She would cherish Egypt and she would cherish her life!

She went through Abdel Hamid's appointment documents from the seventies, and discovered that his highest qualification was a commercial diploma. She thus decided to have him transferred to the archive for a few months, and after that to decide his fate. Was he to remain in the archive, or did his qualifications require a more strenuous job, such as a janitor, for instance? Or maybe an office boy, or ...

Her dreams and wishes grew day after day!

As for Khaled ... Khaled.

He was to be feared.

Khaled knew too much. To cut his throat would be the ideal thing to do. But since the law in Egypt, unfortunately, still criminalizes premeditated murder – even if committed by necessity – she had to think of another way to deal with him. She had to keep her eye on him at all times. That should be easy now. He had registered for a PhD with Professor Muhammad Abdallah. Professor Muhammad would not mind giving her his student if she asked him to!

Since she was now Head of the Department, she could shackle Khaled with bonds he could barely wriggle free from once he had become her PhD student.

And once shackled, he won't open his mouth.

Once Khaled was pinned down, she would calmly contemplate the future. She might need him again, who knows?

She had asked Ramy, 'Do I dare to dream?'

He had said, 'No!'

Where are you now, Ramy, to see me transcending all my dreams, all my aspirations – achieving all I wanted in one shot!

The day of her grand victory. The day that should go down in history, for she was going to change it forever!

She sighed in ecstasy, the likes of which she had never felt before, and sat down at the large desk. She breathed in with pride and joy, looking at her watch. In a few minutes the meeting she was going to chair would start! There was nothing in the world she wanted at this moment. Nothing. There had been one thing she had once wanted – to lose her virginity – and even that wish had come true. Now everyone would flock into her office like a herd submissively following its shepherd. There was justice, then, in this country. There was justice, and the opportunity for growth and excellence.

The professors filed in respectfully, each one congratulating her and singing her praises.

Hanaa was wearing a dark brown suit and a dark red scarf. The tone of her voice had changed slightly. Perhaps it had become a bit higher, a bit more forceful. She was now giving orders, awaiting no reply. The teaching assistants came in, too.

She saw him sitting at the back, guiding his friend Muhammad as usual. He would sit next to him, hand him some water, care for him. This Khaled was very strange. No problem: she'd get to know him better soon enough.

Forcefully, she declared, 'I want to talk to you about a number of topics. First, I would like to say that I'm very happy with this opportunity presented to me by the Dean. I hope that as of today our allegiance is to this institution. Yes. Our allegiance is first and foremost to the university. And I am here to serve the goals of the university. And—'

She was looking at him. He was writing something. Khaled. What was he writing? Her words?

She felt proud. Her eyes met those of Professor Samy. She smiled boastingly and resumed, 'There are some rules that we may all have forgotten. We are here as the patrons of science and knowledge, and the transmission of knowledge is our foremost objective. Therefore, I will be taking a number of measures which may seem very rigid but in fact serve the institution.'

She put on her glasses and started to read out loud, 'First: the professors. I will not permit any secondments abroad at the present time.[2] The reason for this is that delegate professors are always, as we know, negligent of their research: they end up working solely as teachers. When a scholar neglects their research, they die, and they become no different from a school teacher.'

The professors glanced at each other disbelievingly, so she added, 'Any objections?'

She looked around, but no one said a word. No one dared to object. No one was used to objecting. Her question was hollow and meaningless.

She went on confidently, looking from above her glasses at everyone in the room. 'Therefore, scientific research will be given the highest priority among the tasks assigned to professors. Their salaries will be decided accordingly. Their efficiency will be measured accordingly. As for the teaching assistants, I say it now: I will tolerate no private tutoring. If I find out that anyone engages in private tutoring, they are liable to be penalized. Thirdly, concerning scholarships: those who deserve them will get them. Not those who by virtue of social circumstances have better chances in life. Let us together aim at improving the standards of our university and our country.'

Continuous applause broke out. She smiled in ecstasy. Professor Samy got up and said vehemently, 'I'm going on secondment, professor.'

It was an act of defiance she had not expected. Plucking up her courage, she said, 'No, professor. I will not approve your secondment. Egypt needs you.'

His voice gained in pitch and volume as he retorted, 'I will go, professor. And I will get the permission if I have to get it from the Minister himself!'

---

2 In order to supplement their income, many university professors in Egypt take extended periods of unpaid leave to work at universities in the Gulf.

A whisper flitted round the room, while she said again, her voice rising too, 'As long as I'm in this chair, you will not go. The meeting is over for today. Thank you, professors.'

Everyone started walking out. She looked at Khaled opening the door for his friend, and said with the power she now relished, 'Khaled and Muhammad, I would like to talk to you.'

He looked at her. He stared at her, and every time he looked at her, she remembered embarrassing scenes. She reached out to shake hands with Muhammad, saying, 'How are you? And how is your MA?'

He shook hands with her. Her hand lingered in his. He was feeling it, as if he was trying to get to know her better. Then he replied, 'We are lucky to have you as our head of department, professor.'

She smiled. Khaled looked at his watch, then at Muhammad's hand, and said impatiently, 'We should be going now.'

Muhammad let go of her hand and said, 'Yes, we should go.'

Defiantly she stopped him, 'I want you, Khaled.'

He started to help his friend out of the room, then came in again. He looked at her, and their eyes locked. Quietly he said, 'May I sit down?'

She said with pride, sitting down at her stately desk, 'Didn't I say I wanted you?'

He smiled, replying, 'Yes, you did. And I don't know what that means exactly. Forgive me, professor, but sometimes I don't understand you.'

'What were you writing?'

'Your words, of course. We learn from you, professor.'

She said haughtily, 'How are you?'

He turned away from her and replied, 'OK. Especially now, with the advent of the new world order.'

'What do you mean? Are you mocking me?'

'Would I dare?'

'No. You wouldn't. Especially now. You know why?'

He murmured calmly, 'Because now you are my supervisor. If I annoy you, you will raise hell. I may find myself like my *djinn*-obsessed aunt. An aimlessly wandering, homeless fugitive.'

Crossly, she snapped, 'You are mocking me!'

'I just don't understand you. What is it you want from me, professor? How do you want me?'

She opened her mouth, but he went on calmly, 'I know what you want. To secure my loyalty. You're a great leader, professor. That's why I was trying to learn from you. Maybe one day soon the leadership will come to me.'

'Do you have your eyes on my post?! That's what I feared, Khaled. You're ambitious and clever. You have to remain by my side, to help me establish a new order, one characterized by honour, integrity and justice.'

He looked at her, was silent for a moment, then said, 'Will you allow me to speak up, or will you have my head?'

'Speak.'

'You have first to understand the old order before establishing a new one. No leader in Egypt should underestimate the old order.'

'And what is the old order?'

'Exactly.'

'Excuse me?'

'That question puts the order in a nutshell. No one knows. There is no order.'

'I don't follow you.'

'Precisely. We're all so used to not understanding. If we did, it would be the beginning of the end.'

'Ignorance is futility!'

'And bliss!'

'How do you mean?'

'Have you appointed anyone as secretary yet?'

'I will today, or tomorrow. I have three applications, and I know who I want.'

'May I ask about two of the three?'

'Do you know the third?'

'Yes. It belongs to Hend, our neighbour. An excellent girl, and very devout. She helps her parents earn a living. She needs this job more than anyone else. Professor, please take her application into consideration.'

She opened the file and skimmed through Hend's application. Then she commented, 'Her computer skills and knowledge of English are poor.'

'She'll learn fast.'

She looked at him, analysed him, then said, 'What is she to you?'

'I respect her. I appreciate her, and she needs the job.'

'I have another application submitted by the daughter of a colleague. She hopes to get this job to fill her spare time, when her children are at school. He's a well-known professor at the Philosophy Department. If I strengthen our relationship, he may come in useful one day.'

'But you won't take her.'

Amazed, she asked, 'How do you know?'

'Because your allegiance lies with the institution. I have your words here in my notebook.'

'The third one is not poor. Her father is a civil servant, her mother an engineer. She's both good at English and has computer skills. She's smart and cultured.'

He commented, perplexedly, 'But she doesn't need the job. Hend needs it far more. If she can't find work, what will she do? You can't turn your back on someone who needs your help.'

'Khaled. You just pointed out that my allegiance lies with the institution, not with individuals. The university is my proprietor, not the people. As long as the university is my priority, I will appoint whoever is most qualified, not whoever is poorest and neediest.'

He glanced at her, then said apprehensively, as if she had just decided to commit high treason, 'Your allegiance lies with the government, then.'

'I am here for the government!'

'Yes. That's the problem, Professor Hanaa. In Egypt, people don't pay allegiance to the government but to each other. No one knows the government. No one trusts the government. Here we live and work in the shittiest of circumstances, because our allegiance is to each other. The government won't be appreciative. You won't save Egypt by appointing individuals. But Hend would appreciate it.'

'Yes. That's the problem. Allegiance. In other countries, one's allegiance lies with the institution, not with individuals, feelings or favouritism. I'll begin with myself, then.'

He got up, deeply troubled.

'OK. Do you want anything else from me?'

She glared at him and said, 'No private tutoring. You know that now.'

He answered mechanically, 'Yes, of course. It's your call. And democracy? How does it function in this government institution?'

'In its appropriate context, it is beneficial. However, when abused by idiots, it becomes a weapon that backfires.'

'Yes. You're right.'

She smiled sarcastically. 'Of course, you could marry Hend to protect her virtue. She'll make a good wife, too. She'll see to your every need.'

Calmly he replied, 'Yes, that's a possibility. But I ought to pledge allegiance to our institution and the leaders of our institution. Not to a poor girl. Or else, I may never get a PhD.'

'Meaning ...?'

'Usually I don't mean anything. Sometimes I mean a thing or two.'

'You never take anything seriously. I don't understand you.'

'But certainly as my supervisor, you should understand me. In the future, maybe. Congratulations, professor.'

When Khaled had left the room, he was seething with rage at everything. He had simply ignored this tremendous energy within him for years. But now it grew with the anger he felt towards this woman who had given herself to him, then jilted him, as if he meant nothing to her.

No, of course he did not love her. Nor did he want her. But his ego had sustained a heavy blow. He had expected that a woman who had lost her virginity to him would beg him to marry her. He had expected her to cringe with shame at the sin she had committed, not to go on living as if she had only sacrificed an old dish and given it away to the poor.

He was not going to think about her. May God save him from a situation that might threaten his future! Now he would marry Safaa, or someone else. And he, too, would live as if he had never seen the old dish, nor tasted from it.

She had saved him by ignoring him. If she had asked him to marry her, he would have been obliged to do so, and then to divorce her the same day.

Of course, she'd saved him. Now he needed to fast and repent. To run home to Boulaq from the campus, shower with ice-cold water and get some sleep.

For the first time in his life he looked around him. He saw the lights, the shops, the people. The people were everywhere, nothing separating them. There were no borders to their existence, nor to their essence. He couldn't see anything else. The noises did not bother him; the tiny distances separating everyone did not bother him. It was the way people merged into one another, one entity, suffering, laughing, shouting, doing everything simultaneously.

He climbed the old crumbling stairs to his flat. He rang the bell, knowing that his mother would open the door with that look of indescribable joy in her eyes. She always had that look on her face whenever she saw him or his brother. His sister, on the other hand, was not favoured with the same regard; but she didn't work. She studied, made demands, spoke on the phone, while he and his brother worked day and night. He had shouldered all the financial responsibilities since the death of their father four years ago. He was the breadwinner, and was helping his brother with his wedding expenses. He was putting aside part of his own income for his sister. He was also paying the instalments for his flat in al-Haram Street. He paid a lot for others, and only little for himself. He enjoyed great esteem in the eyes of everyone. But, of course, his salary at the university was not even enough to buy meat for a week.

That was why the idea of abolishing private tutoring seemed both naïve and foolish to him. But then Professor Hanaa was nothing but naïve and foolish!

No sooner had he walked in than his mother opened the fridge and took out a covered plate with meat which she had kept for Khaled. She set about preparing lunch.

He sat there absent-mindedly, as he tended to do these days.

Feeling concerned, his mother told him, 'It seems Safaa wants you back, my son. She called Shaimaa yesterday and kept flattering me. But please, don't get back together until she learns to listen to you and to obey you!'

He picked up his spoon and replied, 'Yes, of course.'

'I mean, don't rush into anything. Women are a dime a dozen.'

He played with his food in silence, so his mother resumed, 'I made you some baklava – the kind you like. So you remember, no one makes pastries like your mum, with tonnes and tonnes of sugar! That girl, Safaa, she doesn't even know how to cook. Besides, she's far too dark-skinned. I want you to marry a fair-skinned girl, who also has large breasts, as if she's breast-feeding. That girl doesn't even have a figure!'

He nodded in agreement, then got up. His mother exclaimed anxiously, 'What's wrong, Khaled? Did I upset you? Don't tell me you love her, Khaled. You're a man, my son! She's just a kid.'

He whispered calmly, 'Not at all, Mum. I'm just a bit tired. By the way, tomorrow I'm fasting.'

'Why?'

'I have made a vow. I'll fast a month or two. I'm not sure. Now if anyone asks, I'm not here.'

Then suddenly he asked, 'Is Shaimaa back yet from school?'

Hurriedly his mother replied, 'In her room. Studying. Don't worry, Khaled. Your wish is my command. You're the man of the house, my son. Ever since that big fight she's never late.'

She gazed into his his face and went on beseechingly, 'You work too hard, darling. Especially with Muhammad. You're more than a brother to him. May God reward you for your kindness, my son.'

He answered mechanically, 'I don't do this to get a reward. I do it because he's my friend. You know, once I tried to close my eyes for five minutes, doing nothing. I felt frustrated, powerless, scared. He has to keep his eyes closed forever. No. I'm not doing this for a reward.'

'And the time you spend?'

'It's not wasted with Muhammad. He's my friend.'

Like always, she started reciting prayers for him. He flashed an artificial smile and went to his room.

A moment later, his mother walked in with a plate full of baklava. Khaled's mum was passionate about making baklava, and passionate about eating it. She also hated with passion, and grieved with passion; her emotions always gushed forth like hot syrup pouring across the surface of baklava trapped in its mould.

He finished his classes, thinking of the private tutoring session that was due to begin in half an hour. He had to take his books with him, then get the keys from his drawer in the teaching assistant's room, then …

A voice called from behind him, 'Dr Khaled.'

He turned around to find a short, skinny girl. She smiled and said shyly, 'I'm Lobna. A student in your freshman class.'

Mechanically he answered, 'Hi, Lobna.'

He was hurriedly walking down the hall as he always did while she hurried along, gasping but talking on, 'I wanted some private tutoring in poetry.'

He stopped, looking at her. Then he said, 'You are in your first year?'

Enthusiastically she asked, 'Do you know Professor Hanaa?'

'Of course I know Professor Hanaa. I know her only too well.'

The girl smiled shyly, then said, 'She's my aunt.'

His eyebrows rose in amazement, thanking God Lobna had mentioned this fact before he gave her an appointment for the first lesson.

He answered earnestly, 'I'm sorry. I don't offer private tutoring. It's not allowed, Lobna.'

She whispered beseechingly, 'Please, doctor.'

He answered firmly, 'It's not allowed.'

He fell silent for a few seconds, then continued, 'But Professor Hanaa has done us too many favours. If you need any help, you can always come to me.'

She smiled enthusiastically, shyly, and whispered, 'But …'

He interrupted her, saying, 'For free. I will help you for free.'

'I think I will need more help. Is there any way you can come to give me a private class at home? Please?'

He fell silent for a moment and then said, 'Give me your address, and I will try to come see you once a week, if I can. But I will not charge you for it.'

'Oh thank you, doctor.'

He was suddenly perplexed and asked, 'But how did I never realize before that you are her niece? Very strange indeed.'

'Because Aunty Hanaa told me not to tell anyone. She's very strict and conscientious.'

'Ah, I see. Well, Salam, Lobna. See you soon.'

This was not the first time for him to offer tutoring for free. He had done this frequently since his graduation four years ago. Especially for the children of professors, officers and VIPs.

Hanaa certainly deserved a favour, even though he knew she did not want any. But he was acting more strangely these days. He was acting without thinking, and it worried him.

Leila, Hanaa's sister, was her exact opposite. Her looks were hesitant and confused, her figure huge, her clothes colourful and tight; gold jewellery covered her arms, neck and fingers, and her voice was loud and strong.

She welcomed him as if he were the prodigal son. Like a caged lioness she turned around, in search of her servant, the doorman, the cups, the coffee ...

She motioned him to take a seat, then called for the doorman at the top of her voice through the light-shaft. 'Abdou! You idiot, answer!'

When Leila spied him, she shrieked, 'All right, you son of a bitch. I'll give you a sound beating, and then I'll have Adel hang you by the balls! When I call you, you come instantly!'

Khaled felt very uncomfortable. Humiliation tired and irked him. He sensed how much of their humanity people gave up to survive in the burrows of the poor. How the rich of Egypt had become tyrants. They held everything in their hands, from the daily bread to the whips and the gallows.

He closed his eyes for a moment, then heard Lobna asking tenderly and shyly, 'What would you like to drink, Dr Khaled?'

Before he could answer, Leila said, 'You must have lunch with us.'

He answered with determination, 'I can't.'

She insisted, 'But you must, doctor.'

Provoked by her, he answered emphatically, 'I'm sorry. I have work I must finish.'

She went on enthusiastically, as if she had not heard him. 'Hanaa is coming to have lunch with us today. You must wait for her.'

He was silent for a moment, finding himself surrounded by this weird family.

Sternly, he turned to Lobna, 'I can't. Let's start our lesson now; then I have to go.'

He opened the book. Lobna timidly sat down next to him, and the lesson began.

He had intended to include her in one of his groups. Of course now that was out of the question, otherwise Professor Hanaa would know for sure that he offered private tutoring. The other solution he was considering seriously was to apologize to Lobna and cancel the sessions. Since he was not going to earn anything anyway, and since her mother was heartless and a pain in the neck, it would be better to be rid of her.

For some unfathomable reason, however, he did not want to be rid of her!

He sensed the mother's eyes burning into his back. He knew the eyes of mothers panting for a prospective husband. He had often suffered from them during lessons.

He had never thought of Lobna as a woman. She was the niece of a woman. A woman he had known only too intimately. Or had not known at all.

He heard the doorbell chime, then heard Hanaa's voice, strong but calm. In his mind's eye, he saw her firm, confident look. Hanaa walked in with a foil-covered dish in her hands, saying to her sister, 'This is half a melon I bought yesterday. Couldn't eat all of it. It was delicious. The kids may like it.'

Leila opened her mouth, baffled. Hanaa's avarice and her way of talking always baffled her. She would whisper every night into her husband's ear, 'I know why Hanaa never got married! Who'd be able to put up with her? She's so tough, so tight-fisted, so haughty, so—'

Her husband would agree with her. He hated Hanaa as much as he hated poverty. In fact, he usually avoided being together in the same place with her.

Hanaa smiled, 'How are you, Leila?'

Enthused, Leila replied, 'You know Khaled, the Teaching Assistant at your department? He's in there, in the living room. What a guy, Hanaa!'

Hanaa stared at her, then asked, 'Is he tutoring Lobna?'

'For free! Imagine! Are there still people like that in this day and age?'

Hanaa answered sardonically, 'No. There aren't. He's very kind, generous, giving.'

'How do you know?'

'And very obliging too.'

'He doesn't want to stay for lunch.'

'Is Adel coming for lunch?'

'No, he's very busy.'

She smiled, 'Is he good to you, Leila?' she asked.

Hesitantly she answered, 'Oh yes, very much so. He's the best man in the world.'

Hanaa never found out what Adel did to his wife. She suspected that he humiliated her. She was pretty sure of it. Leila whispered feebly, 'Do you have two hundred pounds on you? I don't want to sell any of the gold. And the household budget has run out. And—'

She glanced at her, then said, 'Of course.'

'I'll give it back on the first of the month, Hanaa.'

'If your brother hadn't conned us out of our inheritance, you wouldn't need to borrow.'

She shook her head in embarrassment. As usual, she was anticipating her little sister's words of reproach, her advice and guidance for economical housekeeping, her objection to squandering, the future, the greedy brother ...

After a while Leila said, 'Lobna is at your department, Hanaa. We want her to become a Teaching Assistant. Take care of her. She does love you. Relatives deserve greater generosity, and she's like your own.'

Hanaa's jaw dropped in disbelief, as if Leila had asked her to sacrifice her honour and prostitute herself. 'Relatives deserve greater generosity?'

'Isn't it so, sister? Adel sometimes says that you're not very obliging. But I said my sister is very helpful, kind and generous.

Hanaa gave no answer. She glared at her sister with outrage and disdain.

Leila held a piece of chocolate which she kept for moments like these, and started nibbling at it in confusion. Gulping down the last piece, she asked, 'Are you upset now?'

'Leila. A feat of generosity that goes against my conscience is not a favour, but a crime. And stop eating chocolate! It's not healthy for you.'

Leila's face flushed, and she replied in confusion, searching for another piece, 'Aren't you a woman? Is there a woman alive who doesn't love chocolate? It's this that helps me survive, my dear. A woman without chocolate must suffer from an emotional vacuum. And you have enough of a vacuum in you as it is. A bit of chocolate helps us get through the bitter days. When you get to my age, you'll understand! There is a time in a woman's life, Hanaa, when nothing helps her but sugar and pastries.'

'I won't discuss this with you. Why do I bother to discuss this with you? You refuse to understand.'

Khaled closed the book, and said with a smile, 'I'll see you on Saturday, Lobna. Do you have any questions?'

She replied enthusiastically, 'Yes. Will you have lunch with us today?'

He looked at her in surprise. 'What does your father do for work, Lobna?'

'He's a businessman. He has a nail factory.'

'Is he coming for lunch?'

'I don't know.'

He answered sternly, 'If he's not coming for lunch, it's not appropriate for me to stay for lunch either.'

She replied with warmth, 'Of course he's coming. You know, Daddy had a horrible accident a month ago.'

'Accident? A car crash?'

'No. Daddy is very successful and strong. And he has many enemies. One day he was visiting a friend of his in Mohandeseen. A robber, or one of his enemies, broke in – I'm not sure. But he shot Daddy and stole all his clothes, and left him lying there. Just like that, all naked and bleeding in that flat.'

Her eyes became moist with tears, and she continued, 'He would have died, if the neighbours hadn't heard the gunshots. But the guy got away.'

Then she whispered through her tears, 'I'm very scared for him, Dr Khaled.'

He almost burst out laughing. It was such a strange story, and he did not understand it. Nor did he know why Lobna was telling him all this. Had she been that affected by it? Was she trying to make small talk with him?

But Lobna's father was a man – how could he describe him? Well, he understood. If Leila had been his wife, he would have done a lot. They found him naked, and shot by another man in a flat. Of course, there was no mention of a lady. Nor of the man who had probably opened fire on his wife and her lover.

He smiled sardonically and said, 'Your father is a very brave man.'

She nodded and said, 'Very. Will you have lunch with us?'

He got up. 'No. But I'd like to say hello to Professor Hanaa before I go.'

He opened the door and his eyes met Hanaa's. He smiled tepidly, and she returned it. As he was walking towards the front door, he said, 'Nice seeing you, professor. Salam.'

Since Professor Hanaa now held the reins in her hands, she was subjected to the same ancient Egyptian rituals by which authority and power are handed over to the decision-makers, with a number of simple symbolic gestures.

Not a month had gone by, and Professor Hanaa's office was overflowing with gifts in the form of calendars, notebooks, pens and letter-openers. Whenever she entered her office, she would sit down expecting to see a new calendar with landscapes, pharaonic pictures or tourist sites. Every month in each calendar had a different theme. When she counted the calendars, she found around five hundred, given by various professors, teaching assistants, students, parents, workers, employees – right down to the office boy, who had brought her a small desk calendar.

Everyone came to visit her, praise her and laud her achievements and policies, her conscientiousness and her respectable personality. When she reminded them that she had assumed office only a month ago, they would enthuse, 'But you made a difference. You are different. You have a conscience. You take the university's interests to heart. God bless you!'

Hands would shake when they shook hers. Tongues would stammer. Eyes would be downcast. And the men and the women were alike in their respect, praise and eagerness to work on reforming the institution and the leaders of the institution.

Her sense of greatness made her intoxicated. It was as sweet as cool fresh water on a hot day. Hanaa was not stupid, and she did not believe all the views and compliments offered by everyone. Yet she was human, too. She felt proud – as proud as a person who had just taken charge of a country and a treasury with millions, leading a people in need of guidance, assistance and knowledge.

Appointing her secretary was a quick and smooth job. She personally supervised the procedures. Rasha understood her tacitly, and was a quick learner. She, the third applicant, was the best one for the job. She appointed her not because she was poor and not because her parents were important. She appointed her because she was the most qualified for the job.

When Professor Maysah came in to extend special congratulations to Hanaa, she was about a month and a half late. As always, Maysah held a handkerchief to wipe her brow. The handkerchief stuck to her fingers, and she wore a blue gown, a blue embroidered veil and many rings, necklaces and bracelets. She wore a tight-lipped smile, and said in an affected voice, sitting down opposite Hanaa, 'Congratulations, Hanaa. You deserve the best.'

Hanaa smiled back and said confidently, 'You too, Maysah.'

Maysah started an endless monologue, as if talking would help her avoid showing the disgust she felt for Hanaa and her haughty manner!

She started bragging about her husband's and her children's achievements, as if trying to direct a message of hatred forcefully at the enemy.

Hanaa guessed at Maysah's aim. She wanted to rub salt into her wounds ... to avoid confrontation like a coward but still to rub it in: *Hanaa, you may be the head of the department, but you're a spinster! No child. No husband.*

When their interview, fought with nuclear, chemical and illegal weapons, was over, Hanaa got up to search for something in her drawers. Maysah suspected she may have been looking for a gun for the final, lethal, shot. Hanaa pulled something out and smiled to Maysah. 'Maysah, please accept this small gift from me.

A watch. I hope this year you look at it before you dismiss class. It seems you don't have one. A lecture is two hours, Maysah, not forty-five minutes.'

Maysah's eyes glared and sparked, her jaw dropped and she seemed to spit fire like a dragon. She didn't touch the watch, but gave a tepid smile and excused herself.

Hanaa laughed out loud, then called her secretary in, saying with aversion, 'Rasha, what do you think of Maysah? Don't you think she's far too fat? Honestly, a woman should take care of her appearance and figure. She is careless both of herself and her research!'

Rasha answered enthusiastically, 'She's not like you, professor.'

Hanaa looked at her sharply and said, 'Ah, Rasha. You still don't understand me. I don't like flattery. Especially not from my secretary. Not from anyone, but definitely not from you. You should be my eyes, not my rose-tinted glasses!'

***

Khaled Abdel Rahman. He was constantly on her mind these days, and she certainly saw him a lot. Wasn't this the way she wanted it to be? Khaled was a bright young man. He was ambitious and worked with rare sincerity. He had been a top student in high school, had learnt the Koran by heart and was the pride of both his family and the entire district of Boulaq. An honourable Egyptian role model.

She smiled, leaning back in her grand leather chair in her office.

Khaled Abdel Rahman! He was now like soft clay between her fingers for her to shape and form. So what did she want from him?

Now that she was at the top of the world, she needed his help from time to time. Nothing more.

His help with what?

Technicalities, like problems with the computer.

She called her new secretary in and asked her to summon Khaled.

She leaned back again in her seat.

Now she held the world between her hands. Now she wanted her lost years. Now, sometimes—

No. She wouldn't think of that. She would live day by day. Khaled's destiny was not decided yet. She might send him to the guillotine, or take him into her arms. Or both!

He walked in hesitantly.

At times, he seemed hesitant and shy. At other times, he was audacious and aggressive. Now he seemed hesitant.

She said firmly, 'I need your help, Khaled.'

He remained standing at the door and replied mechanically, without looking her in the eye, 'At your service, professor.'

She said earnestly, 'I have a problem with the computer. I saved my last lecture on it, but now I can't find it.'

She sat in her chair, exuding confidence.

He seemed to hesitate again, then said, 'May I close the door?'

'Yes, of course,' she replied, getting up and turning on her computer.

He closed the door and took his seat in front of the computer. She, too, resumed her seat, turning the computer monitor towards him. There were only a few centimetres separating them. She sensed his presence in a way that she had never experienced with any man before. He seemed absorbed in the search for the lost file. He was a computer whiz, and he was young. He leaned forward towards the monitor, propping his arm on the desk, and worked in silence.

Her heart beat rapidly, and she felt herself losing control. She desired him as if she were a teenager, but she was in her forties. Her body felt as if it had been revived after years of death. She almost wished it hadn't!

Why now? Why did she allow these absurdities to destroy her now? She feared these feelings, and wished she could uproot her femininity. But she didn't know how.

She was confused by her mixed feelings: feelings of yearning, of guilt and of shame at being a woman, feelings of confidence, strength and the power to get anything and everything she wanted.

And there was also the feeling that she was a vampire sucking the blood of this young man.

It was as if a dormant, forgotten volcano had suddenly erupted and turned her whole life upside down. If only she had not lost her virginity! If only she had kept the lid on the Pandora's box which she was now so keen to explore.

But ... she had the power to get anything and everything she wanted.

Her fingers started drumming nervously on the desk. She looked at him again while he bent over the monitor. Her fingers moved slowly, tracing down his spine, then she whispered, 'Did you find the file?'

He swallowed hard. His hand trembled for a moment, then he froze as if she had bewitched him, as if she had turned him to stone.

He didn't speak or move. He remained still, desire tearing at his gut, his yearning for her rising to the surface. Her fingers still moved down his back. He could feel them.

Suddenly she quivered nervously, and said crossly, 'We have to get married!'

He swallowed hard once more, then whispered hoarsely, 'Excuse me?'

She repeated earnestly, 'We have to get married.'

He drew away from the monitor and looked at her, without saying a word.

'Why are you giving me that look?'

'I'm trying to understand, as usual.'

'There is nothing to be understood. I've thought this over, and I've decided to marry you.'

This intoxicating feeling of power was almost making her lose her mind. Why shouldn't she? Everything and anything was in her hands.

Silence prevailed for a moment, as if he was trying to regain focus and self-control.

In the same sarcastic tone that she was now used to hearing from him, he replied, 'May I ask why you changed your mind, professor? Especially now? Why would you trust me? What if I made this public? I assume you want a secret marriage? Or have I hurt you with the mere thought?'

She said forcefully, 'I want a legitimate marriage, conducted by a marriage official.'

'And you want everyone in the university to know? Your family? The people?'

She burst out vehemently, 'No.'

'Why should I agree to this? Under what threats? Not even a PhD is worth selling myself for. Why should I marry you like this?'

Her jaw dropped in horror. 'Surely you have lost your mind! Never ever forget the limits between us. I only want to marry you in case I may be pregnant. Who knows?'

He almost burst out laughing, then said calmly, 'After three months I think you should know if you're pregnant or not. Are you, professor?'

She said forcefully, sitting down at her desk, 'I am the one who asks questions. Me, not you. You don't question me. I thought this might be a tempting proposition for you. But—'

He stared at her in astonishment, 'Why would it be tempting?'

She didn't answer.

He smiled spontaneously. 'You're right. I'm sorry. You may be pregnant. OK, professor, I agree.'

She smiled victoriously. 'I have a few conditions.'

'I agree to all of them.'

'No one is to know.'

'Of course.'

'Never take liberties with me.'

He looked at her face, then smiled and said, 'Never. I won't.'

'Our relationship will always remain like this. Professor and student.'

'How?'

'You will come to my house from time to time because I supervise your PhD. You will never spend the night with me in the same house after our first week of marriage.'

He opened the door while thinking about her proposal and asked, 'When do we tie the knot? Today?'

She smiled with a touch of tenderness. 'Maybe.'

He had lost his mind. No doubt, he had lost his mind. He didn't want to marry her. What did he want? He wanted her. He wanted to sate this desire that tore at him, which no other woman would be able to quench. An affair, then. For a certain period of time. But it was not an adulterous affair. Yes. He was not committing adultery. She would be his wife. He wouldn't feel guilt or shame or fear. No, he would not.

He burst out laughing, walking next to Muhammad.

'What's got into you?' Muhammad asked in surprise.

'Very weird things are happening to me these days. Something I wanted – now I will get it.'

Muhammad smiled and said, 'Her hand is very soft and tender. Is she pretty, Professor Hanaa?'

He answered mechanically, 'Maybe.'

Muhammad exclaimed, 'What do you mean with "maybe"? You always describe everything to me. Describe her, Khaled. Describe her, then tell me your story with her.'

Flustered, he replied, 'There is nothing to tell. She's off her rocker, as you can see, and she will get what she deserves soon. She's used to loneliness, I think.'

'She is certainly aggressive and fierce with men. Who'd be able to put up with her?'

'I don't know. Some nutcase. Someone who's been living like a sage all his life and wants to go mad for a change, maybe.'

'You sound like you're describing yourself. But you want an obedient woman, don't you? And she wants someone who obeys her. She's like Shajarat al-Durr.[3] I fear she may kill you in the bathroom, pal. She has a passion for history, leadership and power. She'd kill her own mother for the sake of control.'

'Well, thank God, I'm not her mother. And don't worry. I'll never go to the bathroom in her house. I'll be careful, as you advised. Here we are. Salam, Muhammad.'

'There is this ring of happiness in your voice, as if you're expecting something. What are you up to today?'

'I'm going to Alexandria. If my mother asks you about me, tell her that. I told her the same. I'm staying in Alexandria for a week at least.'

'Are you really going to Alexandria?'

'Of course not.'

'Then where are you going?'

'I'm not answering any more questions.'

---

3 Shajarat al-Durr (d. 1257 CE) ruled Egypt briefly in 1250 as sultan and 'Queen of the Muslims'. She ceded power to her husband Aybeg, but sought to regain the throne after her husband married a second wife by assassinating him. In a famed incident, she had him beaten to death with clogs in the bathhouse.

Chapter 4

He stretched out on the bed, breathing in slowly, and relaxed. He folded his arms behind his head and didn't feel like talking. He sensed her presence next to him, fragile, scared, without confidence, like a dove when it has flown inside a house by mistake. Fluttering about and bumping against every surface. He felt extremely full of himself, teaching Professor Hanaa what he had learnt from books, what he had derived from his imagination and his scant experiences. He wanted her. He wanted to feel her trembling in his arms. He wanted to love her as he should, to see her naked body in front of him, to watch her quivering, hesitating, fearing. Everything that made her weak in front of him. For weak she was. But she didn't see her own weakness. She wanted to assert herself, but this time he was the master.

He whispered, kissing her hair, after she had turned her face away timidly, 'I was studying all these past months, professor, so as not to disappoint you. But I think I need further tutoring.'

She looked at him yearningly, shyly. He brought his face closer to hers. 'You can't deprive a student of knowledge, especially if he's your student.'

She whispered warmly, 'I think in this matter you have taught the teacher.'

He cupped her face in his hands and whispered, 'I want to give you a long kiss.'

She swallowed hard, and said in confusion, 'Yes, but then you must go. It's late.'

'And if I stayed with you? If you slept in my arms? What would happen?'

She answered earnestly, 'The doorman, the people, the—'

'Just for today.'

'Maybe just for today. But the doorman—'

'I'll handle him.'

When he woke up, he looked at her. She was curled up, hugging her knees like a little child. She seemed so small, so fragile. He started feeling uncomfortable. Now she would go back to giving orders, setting conditions, demanding obedience. This barrier would always remain between them. A barrier created by circumstances and hierarchies.

But she was his wife.

What did that mean? Why had she married him?

Why all these questions? He was happy. He was contented, free and ecstatic. What ecstasy!

She opened her eyes, rubbing them, then looked at him, saying, 'Khaled, good morning.'

'Good morning to you too, professor. Would you like to eat something?'

She sighed, 'I usually don't have breakfast, but today I will.'

There was a brief silence, as if each of them was expecting something, then he said, 'Ok, so will you make us breakfast? I usually don't eat in the morning either, but today I want to eat with you. What will you have?'

She gaped in amazement, 'You want *me* to make *you* breakfast? You must be kidding!'

He opened his mouth as if about to reprimand her, then checked himself. Suddenly he said, 'The problem is I'm not used to making myself breakfast.'

'And I don't make breakfast for anyone. Especially for one of my students!'

He got up, feigning calmness, 'So we're not having breakfast?'

'You'd rather not have breakfast than to get up and make some? What will you do for lunch and dinner?'

'I don't know. I have never married my professor before. We'll have to wait for lunch or eat out.'

'Or not eat together.'

Putting his clothes on he said, 'That is also possible. I'll be back after lunch.'

Suddenly she said, 'Khaled, wait. I have an idea. I'll prepare lunch, and you can do the dishes. What do you think?'

Feeling incensed he exclaimed, 'Why can't you act like a woman? What's wrong with that? Would you lose your power if you acted like a woman for one day?'

Jumping off the bed she screeched, 'And would you lose your manhood if you did the dishes?'

He stared at her while she brushed her hair out of her eyes. Then he said tenderly, 'Ok, we'll try.'

She was not used to preparing lunch for more than one person. Nor was she used to cooking for more than one person. Nor was she used to seeing more than one person.

She set the table for two, then took the salad she had prepared an hour earlier from the fridge and put it on the table. She slowly brought out the sliced cheddar cheese and the olives, glancing at her watch. He had promised not to be late. He would be here at three.

This man was wreaking havoc on her orderly life. But that was fine. She was happy, even exhilarated at times.

The doorbell rang. She stopped for a second before opening the door. She didn't want him to think she'd been waiting for him all day!

Slowly, she walked to the door and opened it. He smiled at her, not sure whether he should hug her or not. Should he kiss her? Their relationship was semi-formal again, fraught with embarrassment. He felt strangely tense. She asked confidently, 'How are you, Khaled?'

He took a step, but she said firmly, 'Khaled, please take your shoes off. The maid only comes on Fridays and I usually don't allow anyone to come into the house wearing their shoes. I don't want to embarrass you, but I should be able to say things like that to you now we're married.'

He pretended to remain calm, 'Of course. No problem. People usually ask for that because they pray on the floor, so you'd want to keep it clean.'

She looked at him and said, 'That's not the reason. I can pray in my room. Or on the prayer mat. I just like things to be clean and orderly.'

He bent down to take off his shoes. Holding them, he asked, 'Where do I put them?'

'In the cupboard on the left. Second shelf.'

He entered, still slightly amazed, partly discomfited. He placed the shoes in the cupboard, then stood motionless next to it, carrying a package of pastries.

She invited him to sit down. 'Come in, Khaled. What's this?'

He answered anxiously, already anticipating the answer, 'Pastries. You don't like them, do you?'

'I hate them, especially the syrup that makes your fingers all sticky for hours.'

'Is that the only reason for hating them? I can put them into your mouth. In that case you won't need to touch them at all,' he answered in surprise.

As if struck by an unbearable horror, she retorted, 'Khaled, never forget our deal! You are not to be informal with me.'

He smiled and said, 'Ok. I'm sorry. I thought it was my duty to feed you, to kiss you, to hug you, to love you, to ...'

She answered in embarrassment mingled with anxiety. 'Never speak like that.'

He got up and said, 'I took off my shoes and put them in the cupboard. Can we eat now?'

She motioned him to take his seat at the table. He stared at the unfamiliar food. Cheese and cold pasta salad mixed with tuna.

He smiled and started eating silently. She said, 'I usually don't cook. When you live alone, you don't need to cook. You don't really want to cook, especially heavy Egyptian dishes. I hate fats and pastries. I hate all fats and overindulgence. We Egyptians exaggerate everything. Our beauty. Our feelings. Our rights. Food. Sex. As if that were enough to put an end to all our problems.'

Amazed at her long speech he said, 'Now that you are our leader, all our problems are solved. And the Egyptians will start eating tuna and give up sex.'

She scrutinized him, and said, 'You aren't eating. Don't you like the food?'

'I'm not used to it. But it's good. Your sister is totally different from you.'

She said, trying to avoid anything personal, 'Yes. What do you think of her daughter?'

'Lobna is a good girl.'

She replied enthusiastically, 'I like her, too. But I hate her father.'

Curiously he asked, 'Why?'

She looked at him again. 'You're not eating.'

'Why do you avoid talking to me?'

'Because I don't trust you, of course.'

'What has trust got to do with talking? Besides, you have me bound in plenty of chains. I can't escape.'

'I don't trust anyone, period.'

She got up nervously and started stacking the plates together, clearing the table. 'You don't like my food, do you? If you mean to hurt me by not eating, you—'

He interrupted her sternly. 'We're not going to fight now, professor. We can't keep fighting all the time. Do you want me to do the dishes now?'

She nodded, feeling guilty and ashamed. She had mistreated him. If she went on like that, he would leave. And if he left, she'd be back to her loneliness.

She smiled sweetly and watched him holding the detergent, not quite sure what to do with it. He picked up the sponge and put some detergent on it. A lot of detergent.

She said angrily, 'Watch it. You emptied half the bottle. This is expensive stuff. The bottle costs ten pounds.'

He looked at her in anger, dropped the sponge and said crossly, 'I'll pay for it, Professor Hanaa. This lunch is not up to my expectations. Nor up to yours. This farce has to come to an end. What do you say?'

She stared at him, asking, 'What do you mean?'

He walked out of the kitchen, went to the cupboard and took out his shoes in silence. Tensing up, she said, 'Khaled, don't you dare walk out without permission.'

He glared at her challengingly and asked, 'Why not? I won't ever see the day when I allow a woman to give me orders. Not any woman.'

Her mouth gaped in amazement. 'What did you say? You think I'm a woman?'

'Yes.'

'I'm a professor, but you just see me as a woman, and no more. What do you expect of me? I'll show you this woman's strength!'

Indignantly he said, 'You're always threatening me. Always! As if this were the only way you could treat me. Why? Why do you always feel so insecure with me?'

'Because of these ideas of yours.'

He was at a loss, and asked, 'So what do you want now?'

She pondered a while, then said, 'Let's taste those pastries together. What do you think? You told me there was a way I could eat them without my fingers getting all sticky.'

He stared at her as if she had just slapped him. She was totally unbalanced, more so than any other woman he had ever met. He knew that women were by nature fickle. But he had not expected any of this madness.

She plucked up her courage, took hold of his hand and whispered, 'Khaled ...'

He didn't know what to do now, or what to say.

It was a difficult but pleasant week. She was a wild gazelle, untamed by humans, unwilling to mix with people. It was the first time she had slept in the arms of a man. It was the first time someone had left the lights on in the bathroom. She was anxious about that, and worried about the bill. There was a lot that got on her nerves. When Khaled stretched out on the bed fully dressed. When he left the lights on in the kitchen. When he threw leftovers in the bin. When he bought pastries. When he bought cheap fried food from the takeaway. When ...

Since the death of her mother ten years ago, no one had controlled her life. Now, a lot of distress was caused by his presence. Part of it was caused by the fact that she wanted to spend the evening quietly listening to classical music, then to go to bed and sleep. She loved the calm and orderliness, and hated waste and extravagance.

But Khaled was wasteful and young. He wanted to enjoy everything. She appreciated that he did not want her to bear any household expenses. He would buy everything.

She loved his generosity and his manliness at times, but she hated his Middle Eastern mentality and his backwardness. He was generous. And he had a lot of money. How?

His earnings at university? He seemed richer than her.

She watched him watching television – a football game – attentively and zealously. He seemed so young.

Especially when his team won. He shouted out with happiness like a child that had just learnt to ride a bike!

She would watch him as if he were an alien. A man; but she didn't know men. A young man; but she didn't know the young. From Boulaq; but she didn't know Boulaq. She had learnt a lot this week.

What was she doing? She must have lost her mind.

Sitting down beside him quietly she said, 'Tomorrow you leave, then. This week flew by fast.'

He looked at her, flashing an innocent but impish smile, and said, 'I won't say it was the best week of my life. But it was the most exciting week, for sure.'

'What do you mean?'

Leaning his head back on the couch he said, 'Nothing.'

In her strong, commanding voice she said, 'Where did you get all this money? You've given up private tutoring, haven't you?'

He looked at her angrily, 'Professor, you can't make use of anything you find out about me in this house, in my arms, against me at work! That's so beneath you.'

She swallowed hard. She didn't know what would happen as of tomorrow. Was he going to leave her for good? Would he come every now and then? He would leave her soon, no doubt. He must think her selfish and bothersome. That was why she hadn't married sooner: because she only thought of herself.

He may be right. Who knows?

She placed her fingers on his hand while his eyes were still glued to the television. Her fingers travelled up his arm. Then she picked his hand up and moved it to her lips, whispering, 'Will you leave for good tomorrow?'

He looked at her, almost catching his breath. Then he did catch it, for a second, when she kissed his hand tenderly, humbly, lovingly, beseechingly. She kept his hand on her lips, and whispered, 'Don't leave me, Khaled. Not yet. Maybe later, in the future.'

He pulled her hand away and put her head on his chest.

He frowned, but said in bewilderment, mingled with a touch of despair, 'What do you mean with "Don't leave me"? What are you expecting?'

She whispered, kissing his chest tenderly, trembling, flustered, weakened, her voice almost screaming with fear, 'I don't know. But not now.'

He held her even closer, feeling totally bewildered. Their relationship had been clear. This is what he had believed. But now he was not sure he knew what she wanted, nor what he wanted of her. He didn't even know who she was any more.

This fragile woman, who had cast aside all her weapons, had surrendered to him. He didn't know who she was any more.

He hugged her closely, sensing her body clinging to his. He felt relieved, annoyed, confused, hesitant; but most of all he felt an overwhelming longing for her. He didn't ask himself if her actions were premeditated or not. Or if Professor Hanaa intentionally made a show of her weakness at times to strengthen her grip on him. He was not sure. But after a while he sometimes suspected that every move by Professor Hanaa was carefully calculated. Spontaneity was not one of her prominent traits.

She sat in her room with his arms wrapped around her. She remained silent. So did he, until she said nervously, pulling away, 'Despair. Oh my God. I hate despair.'

She started rubbing her fingers nervously, and said, 'When you leave tomorrow, will you want to come back again?'

He said decisively, 'Of course. You're my wife, professor, not my lover. I'll come, probably the day after tomorrow.'

She felt his ribs touching her, threatening her, warming her, scaring her ...

With a touch of hopelessness she asked, 'Why don't you talk to me?'

'About what?'

'About yourself, your family, your ambitions.'

He was about to say something, then just asked, 'And you?'

'I want to talk with you.'

She talked until the morning, as if she had never talked to anyone before. She told detailed stories about her father's illness and death, and her mother's; details about the illness, about how her sister-in-law had stolen her mother's jewellery out of the cupboard the day she died; how her brother had cut ties with his siblings and seized their inheritance at the instigation of his wife; how her sister lived submissively with an unfaithful, tyrannical husband; how she hated the dominance and power of the rich and her sister's attitude towards the poor; how she dreamt of justice. She went on and on for hours, like a hose that had not poured water for years whose tap he had suddenly turned. She fumed and raged and blushed while he watched in silence.

She sighed, as the first shimmer of morning brought light into the room. 'I hope I didn't bore you with my stories.'

He smiled, laying his head on the pillow. 'Of course not.'

'Now, you tell me about yourself!'

He whispered, pulling her down on the bed, 'Can we get an hour's sleep, and then I tell you everything?'

She shrugged nonchalantly. 'Yes. We can.'

She turned her face away. He put his arm around her waist and whispered, 'You didn't tell me about your life in the States. How long did you stay there? Did you like it?'

She swallowed hard, taken utterly by surprise, the ghost of Ramy appearing in her mind's eye. She didn't utter a word.

He tried again, 'Did you love someone in the States?'

She answered nervously, 'Of course you would think that any girl travelling alone is bound to fall in love and have an affair and go astray and all that ...!'

He fell silent for a moment, then said, 'I don't know. I wouldn't allow my sister to travel alone. Nor would I want my wife to travel alone, either. But you're different.'

She smiled sardonically. 'I'm your wife, remember?'

'You must have loved someone. Didn't you fall in love with anyone all these years?'

She answered with a touch of bitterness. 'I don't want to talk about this.'

This last statement was enough to fuel his curiosity and jealousy.

Sitting up, he let go of her waist and asked, 'Did you love someone before?'

She looked at him then said forcefully, 'Once. Yes. I was in love with someone at university. Not in the States.'

He hadn't expected her answer. She didn't deny it. She didn't evade him. But why would she fear him?

Her words had no impact upon him. He had expected to flame up with rage, but he didn't. He couldn't imagine that her relationship with her colleague had gone beyond words. He knew from her trembling and confusion that her first love had not even kissed her.

Even Safaa was more experienced in kissing than Professor Hanaa.

He said quietly, feeling slightly guilty because he had broached this topic with her, 'Why didn't the idiot marry you?'

'He couldn't,' she said scornfully.

He stared at her disbelievingly. 'What, was he married?'

'No.'

'Was he poor?'

'No.'

'What then? Why couldn't he? He couldn't get married?'

Turning her face away so he wouldn't see the pain etched in her features, she said, 'He couldn't. He was a Christian.'

His jaw dropped in bafflement. The nitwit had wasted her life loving a man she could not possibly marry …

He whispered, afraid of her answer, 'Do you still love him?'

She stared at him incensed, then asked, 'Am I acting towards you as if I still loved him? Do I seem to you like I still loved him? No, Khaled. I don't love him any more.'

He watched the sun's rays flooding into the room, then said, 'I'll hold you for a moment, then I have to go.'

She nodded.

Chapter 5

He had not experienced these feelings of satisfaction and exultation in a long time – since his childhood probably. Since the death of his father, he had only grunted under the weight of his enormous responsibilities and his lingering urge to move on, like a camel trudging through the desert.

But the dealings of fate are unexpected.

His father had entreated him on his death bed, 'Take good care of your siblings, Khaled. You are the oldest, Khaled. You are the father when I'm gone, Khaled.'

If only he had known the amount of pain and loss Khaled would feel once he was gone. His father had been his friend and his anchor. After his death, he gradually came to know his mother, his sister and his brother. He hadn't been close to his mother before. Her efforts had been focused on providing his father with comfort, on cooking, on cleaning the chandeliers and into the corners.

After his father's death, she had vowed allegiance to the new king. He had become her life.

His father had died at a strategic moment, right after the final exams of his final year at university. He had to find work and start planning from the moment of his father's death. From the moment he shook hands with those coming to pay their condolences. He had known that his world had turned upside down, and that it was his responsibility to turn it back the right way up.

But he was happy now.

He wasn't going to attempt to understand the situation.

He was happy. Everyone could see that there was a fresh gleam in his eyes. It was an expression of relaxation, contentment and excitement. A lot of excitement. No demands, no complications, no interference, no exploitation, no tears, no dealing with the cunning of a girl who wanted to possess him like Safaa did. There was no girl who wanted to suck his blood. No girl who expected a dowry and a wedding gift,[4] who expected him to visit her family and buy her mother a Mother's Day present. No girl for whom he had to wait patiently until she would allow him – and only when she invited him – a kiss or a touch or more, who would ask him to wait, and then ...

No. Everything was moving with the spontaneity of Adam and Eve just after the Fall, when the scents of Paradise were still in their nostrils.

His mother watched him, then said with a smile, 'You seem happy, Khaled. Any news from Safaa?'

He didn't want to explain himself, nor to submit to an investigation.

He smiled back and said with childlike enthusiasm, heading for his sister's room, 'What do you think, Mother? I'll buy you dinner.'

He entered his sister's room; she was sitting at her desk fiddling with a few papers, daydreaming. He asked with brotherly warmth, 'Shaimaa, are you studying? What would you like to eat today?'

---

4 In Egypt, a man is expected to provide a flat, a dowry and an engagement gift to his bride. The flat is usually a new one that he owns or that his parents have bought for him. The dowry depends on the status of the family and is usually an amount of money that the future wife's family uses and may add to, to buy furniture for the flat. In the past the engagement gift was usually a set of gold jewellery, but it is becoming more and more common to give a diamond ring.

His mother answered hurriedly, 'Grilled kofta and kebab.'

Shaimaa smiled and said, 'I'd like a burger.'

He grabbed his keys, put them in his pocket and repeated, 'Kofta, kebab and a burger!'

His mother said swiftly, 'God bless you, son.'

He smiled and walked out of the door, feeling once again like a carefree child. He did not have to find his way around in dark alleys, did not have to be patient and endure, did not have to be careful. He was a child brimming with the immense energy of longing and love of life.

When he had gone, his mother pursed her lips and said to Shaimaa, 'Your brother is so kind. All this love and generosity will end up going to someone else, and then he'll forget us completely. You'll see. A man like that, with such tenderness, will find himself around another woman's little finger in no time. I don't trust this girl Safaa, Shaimaa.'

Shaimaa replied angrily, 'But he is duty-bound to take care of us. We come first, not his wife!'

Weary of her daughter's naivety, the mother answered, 'Study, my dear. May God guide you on to a good path.'

When Khaled returned with the food, he was smiling to himself. He had just spent eighty pounds of his father's monthly pension, while Professor Hanaa called for allegiance to the institution and the government. May God keep her as a boss in the government since she does such a good job of it!

How wonderful this feeling of power, victory and ecstasy was! She was capable of anything and everything. She was happier than she had ever been before. Songs, even colours ... everything was more beautiful and delicate. She had never known such emotional fulfilment before, nor had she even imagined its full scale.

He usually came every day or every other day. He would talk to the doorman now. Khaled had told him everything, and the man had promised Khaled not to breathe a word. Yes, he had bribed him. But she didn't ask, nor did she care.

As of this moment, this moment of victory, she would write her history. For history is only written for the great. Her life was in her hands, and she had full control of it. She had full control over everything. How wonderful it was for a woman to be in control of her destiny! No, she was not doomed to eternal solitude. She would not remain the poor professor. She was the head of the department, she was not alone and she was capable of doing anything and everything she wanted.

She was not stupid. She was ambitious, but not stupid. She knew that her relationship with Khaled was transient. Sooner or later, it would come to an end. But this did not bother her at all. She had sipped from the cup of love, and that was enough for her. She would live for success, for research, for scholarship, as she had always wanted to. But now even scholarship had a different taste: it was sweet and enjoyable.

She was careful in dealing with him, and he respected her wishes.

She would sometimes meet him by coincidence at her sister's house where he was helping Lobna. She would give him a pretentiously formal smile, and he would return the smile. They never spoke much.

Whenever Professor Maysah met her, and scrutinized her as if undressing her to inspect her heart of hearts, Hanaa would smile confidently. Maysah would say slyly, 'Hanaa. We're going on vacation to Sharm el-Sheikh tomorrow. My husband and I. Just the two of us.' She would then add with a smile, 'Another honeymoon. I told him we were too old, and the kids all grown. But he insisted we go together. Just us. Next time, God willing, you have to join us, Hanaa.'

Hanaa smiled back, overwhelmed by a new feeling she was unfamiliar with: a feeling of confidence and pride. She said, 'Yes, of course. God willing.'

Their eyes locked. Hanaa's eyes were brimming with contentment. They were shining in a way Maysah did not understand. Maysah walked out of the office, leaving Hanaa sitting on her grand leather chair. She leant back and sighed. She had envied many women. In the past, words like these would often have hurt her. Her feeling of grief at her wasted life had often stung her. Bitterness had lingered in her throat, and would remain with her as she ate, as she worked, as she looked at herself in the mirror. A few days before she turned forty, she had come to hate the mirror. She had come to hate her body, her femininity. The bitterness had taken on a more aggressive and more dangerous form. But now –

She sighed again, hugging herself proudly. Now she felt sorry for everyone else. All other women. Now she felt proud and relaxed. Who was Maysah's husband? Who was he? Did Maysah ever feel what she felt now?

There was no other woman on the surface of the earth who felt what she experienced when she was between his arms.

There was no other woman on the surface of the earth whose femininity had matured and bloomed like hers.

He was the first man in her life; she had not known much about men. He was all the men she had not known; and he had to be, since she did not have the time or the energy to know them all.

However, all of this was not going to make her lose control. She was still writing her history, still holding the pen.

That was the difference between her and Maysah. Maysah was the follower of a man, whereas she herself was the leader of one.

She was the leader of all.

She was used to seeing him, and didn't like having to wait for him. He was never very late.

But problems were unavoidable, and they were usually caused by people. That is why she had hated people ever since she had been little.

The first problem was her sister, who was sad, dim, had trembling hands and always looked as if she had been crying for months.

Her sister's appearance bothered her. She asked her if there was a problem, and her sister answered in a tired voice, 'Nothing.'

She knew that Leila was miserable with Adel, and that she hated him passionately. But Leila's silence did not hold for long. One Saturday morning, she was banging on the door to the family home, Hanaa's home. Carrying her suitcase, she screamed, 'He's left me! He's left me, Hanaa.'

Although Hanaa had expected this, she had never said a word. She had tried to preserve her self-esteem by not speaking up. It was only natural for Adel to tire of his wife and to throw her out. It was natural for him to marry a younger woman and wash his hands of her. She had known, and she had not spoken. A sense of sadness overcame her because she also realized that she couldn't meet Khaled. She wouldn't meet him for a long time – for as long as Leila was in her house.

She had never seen her sister in this state before, and she wasn't comfortable seeing all this weakness. Her sister expressed herself very explicitly and in a very exaggerated manner. She would scream with every day that passed, but no one bothered about her, neither her children nor her husband. She would blame her bad luck and smoke like a chimney, as if she were trying to burn herself up. She would swallow tranquillizers and scream for hours. Hanaa felt sorry for her at first, but the smoke started to irritate her. Her sister's getting used to someone else helping around the house was starting to irritate her, too. She would eat and simply leave the plate on the table. She would smoke and stretch her hand out, waiting for someone to fetch the ashtray. Whenever she came into the room, she would leave a trail of havoc in her wake.

Hanaa started to pray to God that Leila's husband would show up. She started using a lot of air fresheners. In spite of Hanaa's loss of patience, Leila was still screaming on and on and complaining about her life.

One night she called out in the dark, 'Hanaa?'

Hanaa came out of her room drunk with sleep, and said, 'I have to go to work tomorrow, Leila.'

Her sister was wailing like a dying cat. She whispered, 'Do you have any sympathy for me? Do you know why he left me?'

She went to her, fearing the force of these emotions, fearing the dependency of a human being that could reach such limits. Her sister's wailing shook her. She trembled, sitting down by her side, unable even to touch her, until her sister started banging her belly viciously. 'Look at me. Look at me! I'm fat. Fat. I wish I could cut myself up into pieces. Of course he had to leave me. Look at me!'

Hanaa swallowed hard. She impulsively grabbed the hands of her sister, who resisted, shouting, 'You don't understand anything. You don't understand anything!'

She whispered in pain, 'Maybe I do understand. Maybe I understand better than you think.'

'I'm a woman, Hanaa. A woman is condemned by nature and her body. She is a captive of her treacherous body. This treacherous body takes but gives nothing. Our mother always said, 'A woman never does a thing of her own free will. She has no will'. A man sows a child in her, the child grows in her and she is absolutely helpless and hapless. Then her body wastes away, and she's absolutely helpless and hapless. The body burns up like mine is burning, and she's absolutely helpless and hapless. When you turn fifty like me, you'll understand. I know my femininity has perished. My period has stopped. This flush burns my cheeks, and I eat and eat. I eat all the time!'

'Leila, please, calm down.'

'He was bound to go in search of a woman. I'm not a woman any more. Do you understand? Our bodies and our nature control us. We're weak, absolutely weak.'

Hanaa answered back challengingly, 'No. We're not weak. Get a grip on yourself. For your children's sake.'

'They don't want me. They want their father's wealth. Do you know what he said? He said, "I don't want you any more. You can stay in the house if you want, but I don't want you." '

Hanaa felt like she was choking, and a strange sense of weakness came over her.

'You have to take it easy. Please!'

The wailing did not cease. So Hanaa left the room, picked up the phone and called Sameh, her nephew. No answer. She called her niece. No answer. She called Adel, her brother-in-law. No answer.

She tried again. No answer.

The wailing was frightening. She could handle the situation, of course. She would handle it. She didn't need anyone. But if only there were someone she could call.

She dialled a number and heard his voice asking surprisedly, 'Professor Hanaa? What's wrong?'

She whispered hoarsely, 'Leila. I'm worried about her. I think she needs a tranquillizer or maybe even needs to be hospitalized. Khaled, can you help me, please?'

He answered immediately, 'Yes, of course. I'll come immediately and bring a doctor with me.'

He must have felt his ego being boosted when she asked him for help. No doubt he thought she was as weak as her sister believed all women to be.

She picked up the phone again and tried her brother-in-law's number. This time he answered. He was surrounded by noise and didn't know who was calling him. That was his fault. He should have looked at the number before picking up.

Adel had a nickname for every person. Every number had a name, and Hanaa's number would flash the name 'Dracula' on to the screen.

She hissed angrily, 'Your wife is a wreck, and I—'

'She's not my wife any more. I told her if she left the house I'd divorce her. And I did!' he interrupted her curtly.

She fumed, 'The mother of your children, then. She needs her children and a doctor!'

'What do you want from me?'

'To come over here now, so we can talk.'

'There is nothing to be talked about.'

'Adel. You come here now, or I'll disgrace you. You know, I don't give a damn about anything!'

The line went dead. She knew he would come. She wanted him to come so she could slap him with such force that it would leave its mark on him forever.

She closed her eyes, almost eaten up by her anger, while her sister's wailing went on and on.

She opened her eyes to the sound of the doorbell chiming. She opened the door to find Khaled with a doctor.

He looked at her worn-out face, her nightgown and her tousled hair. He smiled without saying a word. He was not much better off. He was wearing a wrinkled shirt and jeans. The doctor went into the room, while she felt embarrassed at her sister's wailing.

He put his hand involuntarily on her shoulder and waited in anticipation. She was on the verge of breaking down, but she didn't.

'She'll be OK, Hanaa.'

He had said 'Hanaa'!

She didn't have the energy to dispute it.

He knew Leila's problem, and she felt ashamed that he knew. She wished she were surrounded only by strong women.

He let go of her shoulder and looked at the doctor coming out of the room, asking, 'Is she all right now?'

'She'll fall asleep in a few minutes. She needs treatment. Can she come to my office tomorrow?'

Hanaa nodded, and started fumbling for her purse, but Khaled said hurriedly, 'This way, doctor,' and showed the doctor to the door, pulling some money from his pocket at the same time.

When he opened the door, the doctor ran into Adel.

Her heart pounded. Trying hard to control herself, she said, 'Come in, Adel. This is Khaled, my student and friend.'

He smiled coldly, not really caring who the young man was.

He was in his fifties, bulky, with large features. His nose gave the impression that he was kind and simple. He was neither.

As soon as Adel entered with Khaled, she thundered in an ice-cold voice, 'You do this to her, for a younger girl? After all these years? When she put up with all your faults?'

He answered carelessly, 'That's my right! I don't want her. God granted us the right to divorce.'

Khaled was looking on silently, not fully understanding what his wife was aiming at or fishing for.

She said in her icy voice, 'You're disgusting!'

He yelled in her face, 'Watch it, Hanaa. If your folks didn't teach you manners, I will.'

Before Khaled could say a word, she had raised her hand and slapped Adel's face with full force, screaming, 'You want to teach *me* manners, you ill-bred lout, you?!'

For a moment he was stunned, then he was about to grab her, but Khaled intervened. He stood between them, saying, 'That's enough. It would be better for you to leave.'

Trying to resist, the man growled, 'I'll kill you, Hanaa. You'll see. I'll—'

Khaled interrupted him, gripping his hands, 'Leave. Now.'

He pushed him towards the door, opened it and said, 'We'll talk tomorrow.'

She stood rooted to the spot, a smile of victory on her face.

Khaled pushed him through the door and closed it while the man kicked the door, yelling and cursing.

Khaled looked at her in anger and amazement. Then he asked, 'Why did you do that? He'll never take her back. Is that what you want?'

She answered calmly, sitting down on the couch, 'He won't take her back. He was never going to. I feel so relieved. Do you think I broke his teeth? Oh how I wish I'd broken a few of his teeth. Oh, Khaled. You have no idea how I longed to do that. For twenty years, I've been wanting to do that.'

'To slap a man?'

'*That* man.'

'So you just wanted me here to protect you in case he hit you? Or was it to teach me a lesson?'

She said hurriedly, 'Don't even compare yourself to him. You're not like him.'

He whispered, sitting down next to her, 'Oh, Hanaa. You do think I'm stupid. All night you've imagined yourself in your sister's shoes, imagining yourself killing me, slapping me, ruining my future.'

She looked at him challengingly, 'I don't think of you all the time. I have a lot on my mind. I'm the head of the department, remember?'

'But you're a woman. You feel everything a woman feels.'

'Don't ever say that.'

'That you're a woman?'

'That I'm weak.'

'I didn't say you were weak. I said you had feelings. To feel is not necessarily a weakness.'

He suddenly burst out laughing. 'Did you see his face when you slapped him? My God. You're crazy.'

'What did you say?'

He looked at his watch and said, 'It's five a.m. Don't you think your sister will sleep another hour or two?'

'Khaled!'

'I miss you.'

She whispered longingly, 'So who's crazy then?'

'You and me both, of course.'

'Khaled. You haven't taken off your shoes. Please. Take off your shoes.'

'I thought we had moved past that.'

In response to the pressure exerted by Hanaa and other people, Sameh and Lobna came to make up with their mother and take her home. It was an embarrassing and uncomfortable situation. Leila seemed unaffected, as if she did not want them any more. Nor did her children seem bothered. It was an ugly situation, which Hanaa did not appreciate. But she felt good about Leila's return home – and the return of her home to her. She felt good about her return to independence and freedom.

She didn't hear from Adel. He didn't want his wife. He had left her the house, a monthly allowance, and had drowned himself in his new love affair. He had left her with her children, her servants, her doorman, the big apartment, the expensive furniture. Leila, however, had wanted no one but him, and now cared only about her humiliation and shame, that killing feeling of helplessness.

There were the days after the calamity, and the days before. The days after the calamity for Leila were taking a new form. Leila had lost everything in a few moments, in a few crucial moments of her life. The most significant thing she had lost was her self-esteem – as a human being, not just as a woman. After a while, the tranquillizers became ineffective. Her children avoided her so that they wouldn't have to listen to her complaints about her life and her betrayal. It was as if the world had deserted her. Weeks later she was a regular patron of the nearby mosque. She attended religious lessons, wore the veil and spent most of her time reading the Holy Koran and religious books. She went to Mecca for the minor pilgrimage,[5] and a few months later she went for Hajj.

When Hajja Leila came back, she had gained so much from religion that it was as if she had put on a magical robe which bestowed enormous power upon her. People's perception of her changed; and Hajja Leila became a religious scholar, who spent all her time in the mosque, or with the sisters, or in prayers or reading religious books. The veil and the pilgrimage had changed the look of disdain in people's eyes.

Within four months Leila had become a totally different person. She had renounced the world, her children and everything else for religion.

When Hanaa visited her and entered her room, she observed a pride in her eyes that she had not seen before. She observed confidence, a peaceful surrender to God. Leila whispered calmly, 'I don't see myself as a woman now, Hanaa. Rather as a spirit in God's hands. He is the Supreme Avenger.'

Hanaa looked at her with misgiving. She didn't know whether Leila's involvement with religion was her own way of finding and asserting herself or whether it was a true desire to be more pious. No, Hanaa never knew the reality of Hajja Leila. However, the pilgrimage had raised Leila's prestige among her neighbours, family members and the people on the street. Even the doorman had become more obedient. As if her power inspired them with awe and forced them into obedience. She had become a devout woman, mother and sister in religion. Gradually she mastered

5 The minor pilgrimage (Umrah) to Mecca can be performed at any time of the year. The greater pilgrimage (Hajj) must be performed at a set time during the lunar month of Dhu al-Hijjah. It includes more intricate rituals and culminates in the Feast of Sacrifice (Eid al-Adha), the highest holiday in the Islamic year.

the religious lessons and started preaching herself. It was as if religion had become a weapon in her hands, just like education and money. It was a powerful weapon, and far more effective, for it scared and inhibited men.

Even Adel. He came to visit her from time to time, to give the children their pocket money. The servant would tell him that Leila was praying in her room. He would wait in disinterest and slight discomfort. He did not hide his disdain for her. But one day he saw her coming out of her room carrying a commentary on the Koran, the *Tafsir al-Jalalayn*, and wearing a white gown and a white headscarf. She did not look at him, but muttered words he could not hear, mostly invocations. With a show of disinterest, but obviously tense, he said, 'Don't you dare curse me, Leila. God won't answer your prayers!'

She smiled sardonically and said, 'And why should you be afraid, Adel?'

'You mean you are cursing me?'

She whispered, looking at him, 'The Supreme Avenger.'

He shouted nervously, 'As a reward for all that I have done for you, you go and curse me?'

She made no reply. Then she looked at her watch and said, 'Excuse me. I have a lesson at the mosque. Then evening prayers. Make yourself at home, Adel.'

With the pen of religion, Leila started to write down her history for the first time. She was determining her own destiny. It was a powerful pen, with wide-ranging impact.

Chapter 6

Rising from her desk, she said forcefully, 'Show him in.'

He opened the door with a smile that burst with enthusiasm and vitality, and said, 'Good morning, professor.'

'Good morning, Khaled.' Her tone was serious.

When at her desk, her tone was always more authoritarian, more challenging; she was almost another person. He was never comfortable when she was there at her desk, but he was also very impatient and he wanted to give her something. He wanted to give it to her this minute!

He sat down rather nervously and brought out a gold chain with a gold pendant in the form of a Koran. 'I was just thinking, we got married without me getting you a gift, so ...'

He held out the chain to her and said gently, 'Your wedding present, professor. It's not much, but I hope you like it.'

She took it from him, looked at the large Koran, gauged its weight in the palm of her hand and then said, 'This must have cost your whole pay cheque.'

He smiled without speaking. She looked at him intently, not knowing what to do, what to say. It was as though someone had placed an unknown child in her arms and she didn't know what to do with it. Holding the necklace she enquired, 'Is this a bribe?'

'No,' he said calmly as if he had expected her question.

'You want to end this relationship peacefully?'

Chuckling slightly, he replied, 'No. No, I don't. I just want to give you a gift. Has no one ever given you a gift before?'

Her whisper held a tinge of despair, 'No, no one's given me a present for a long time ... a long time.'

He got up, slowly locked the door, drew near to her and gently whispered, 'I want to see it on you. Can I help you put it on?'

'No,' she said emphatically.

'When can I see you?'

In the tone of someone who had found him out, she said, 'Ah, I get it. You're trying to make me fall in love with you, Khaled.'

He looked at her, headed towards the door and opened it. 'I don't need to try, professor.'

'You think I'm in love with you? Is that what you think?!'

'Will I see you today?'

'You haven't answered my question.'

'I don't want to answer it.'

'Ok. Yes, you'll see me today. And don't buy any pastries. I won't eat them.'

The idea of the gift disturbed her, and made her exceptionally uncomfortable. What was she supposed to do when someone gave her a gift? What was the right thing to do now? Buy him a gift?

No one even remembered her birthday. She usually spent it sitting on her bed under her luxurious blanket watching an old movie and drinking mint tea. Sometimes, she would eat half or even a whole French gateau. She would wait for the break of dawn. Sometimes her sister remembered her birthday; usually she forgot it. She usually prepared herself months beforehand and thought about what kind of gateau she would have that year, what film she would watch, what bed linen she wanted ...

Then along came this man, and in a second, with nothing leading up to it, he gave her a Koran pendant made of gold. What did he expect?

Confusion and unease. If she bought him anything, what should it be? This very day, before he came to see her, she had to buy him a present.

She did not have time today. Tomorrow, then.

As soon as he arrived, she said nervously, 'I'm sorry, Khaled. I haven't had time to buy you a gift yet. Perhaps I'll get it tomorrow.'

He looked at her in astonishment. Hurriedly she explained, 'I'll get you something in return. Don't worry, I will.'

Laughing, he exclaimed, 'I don't ever want you to return it. Don't you dare ever give me something in return, never!'

She looked at him defiantly, 'Why?'

Indifferently he said, 'No reason.'

'Is it normal for you to give gold jewellery to women?'

'Well, it is normal for me to give gold jewellery to my wife. Isn't that as it should be?'

'And your wife doesn't get you a gift in return?' she asked in a challenging tone.

'Never!'

'Because she's a woman, and doesn't work, and is dependent on you?'

Smiling, he calmed her down. 'It's a gift! Why are you giving it so much thought? It's just a gift. What's the problem? Professor, are we going to spend what's left of our time together thinking about duties and rights and women, women's rights and the purpose of the gift?'

She did not utter a word.

She was thinking. She had spent the night thinking about the gift and how it had stung her and awakened her and moved her and pained her, how it ...

She was not at all stupid. Things were getting out of hand. It seemed that it was no longer she who was weaving her story with Khaled. Maybe now he was, or maybe someone else. But she was not in control of the story. She was no longer the one who wrote history.

So long as he had given her a gift, she was not the one who wrote history.

And since she had been so affected by the gift, she was definitely not the one who wrote their history.

This was a new phase in her life, and she was not sure if she relished the wheels of renewal and innovation which he had set in motion.

Puffed up with pride, she sat at her immense desk ordering tea and coffee and sensing the power oozing from her – the very essence of authority, the ability to do anything and everything. First of all, she was pleased with her choice of secretary. The girl understood Hanaa and was quick-witted and energetic. She was the perfect choice. Moreover, she was well dressed and serious about her work.

There was much rot that needed to be removed from within the walls of the university, and so far there had been no one to help her. There was so much mediation, favouritism and manipulation involved even in the department's entrance exam, and the final exams were not much better. Everyone 'made do'; no one was squeamish about accepting an expensive gift, an invitation to a dinner and belly-dancing show on a Nile cruiser or spending a vacation on the Mediterranean coast. The university salary was just a symbolic gesture on the part of the government to show its appreciation for the professors' great efforts. Meanwhile the professors had to earn their daily living in their own way; there was a kind of indifference to, and sorrowful forbearance of, humiliation and injustice. However, she was there now and would change everything; she would make many enemies, but she would change everything. She herself would supervise the department's entrance exams and thus ensure that only those who deserved it would be accepted into the department. As for grants, once again she had a great number of choices.

Who, then?

There was the grant to America, which should go to someone hard-working and ambitious. The Dean wanted to give it to Salma el-Selemi, the daughter of a famous professor who had recently been elected head of Gezira Sporting Club. He was a helpful man; in other words, he was not selfish. Helpful, in Egypt, means that he was more than ready to help anyone wealthy and influential and to facilitate life for those with money and power.

She was in a difficult situation, caught between appeasing the Dean and going against her conscience, and arousing his wrath while he was the be-all and end-all at university. He was the all-powerful man.

She needed to think about it calmly.

Stretching in her chair, she called her secretary.

She had trained her secretary to be obedient, to relay to her any news she heard, any whispers or gossip exchanged, and to monitor all the other professors' letters and emails.

This did not in any way trouble her conscience; it was a legitimate right for her to know her enemies.

She had not seen Khaled for three weeks. She did not want to see him. At the start of the week, when she did not call him, he had called her; and rather formally she had informed him that she was busy. He did not call again. The issue with Khaled had begun to worry and confuse her; and since she was busy with so many things these days, she would wait before dealing with it.

She asked Rasha, the secretary, to come in. She told her to sit down, then asked forcefully, 'Did you go on the departmental trip to Alexandria like I asked you?'

Smoothly and swiftly she replied, 'It was a lovely trip. Things seemed peaceful and nobody complained about any of your resolutions; all the professors constantly spoke well of you and commended the department's achievements since you've become head.'

Rather impatiently she snapped, 'Rasha! What's wrong with you? You always understand me. I don't want flattery! You know full well what I want to hear.'

Slowly Rasha continued, 'Professor Samy was talking to Professor Maysah a lot and they stopped talking every time I was nearby.'

'And Maysah, who else was she talking to?'

She thought for a moment then said, 'To everyone. She was also laughing with everyone.'

'And Khaled?' she asked, staring Rasha directly in the eyes.

She considered for a time then said, 'Professor Maysah, Professor Samy, his friend Muhammad, Ibrahim and most of the students and demonstrators except for Salma.'

'He doesn't like Salma?'

'He doesn't like her at all. He spent most of the time making fun of her and she was extremely angry with him.'

Looking intently at Rasha she asked, 'Do you think he poses a danger?'

'Who? Khaled?'

'Yes, Khaled.'

Once again she thought for a minute then said, 'He's well liked. I don't know, maybe – but of course you can control him and warn him if necessary.'

Annoyed she said, 'Of course. That's enough, Rasha. Now I want to see Professor Muhammad.'

Professor Muhammad was a respectable person and she admired him and his morals; of course he was also a 'helpful' person – but at least he helped rich and poor alike.

When Professor Muhammad appeared, she asked him what he thought of the changes she was trying to make to the department. He commended her, putting her mind at ease and salving her conscience. Then she asked his opinion about the grant that she had the funding for, to which he replied that he would rather not get involved. Quickly she said, 'But you have to get involved. I don't want to give it to Salma. We both know how she came to be appointed and we both want the grant to be of benefit to the university. I need you to back me if I am to face the Dean; I need the votes of professors like you.'

He felt cornered. 'I don't want to oppose the Dean.'

'Neither do I', she said earnestly. 'I don't want that to happen. But naturally you don't want to oppose my wishes.' Her tone was ominous; it conveyed a threat that was implicit yet extremely direct and forceful. He understood and started to give in. 'What do you need from me?'

'To put forward another name. Then, I go to the Dean with it and tell him it's the department's choice and I can do nothing about it.'

'So fake democracy is the order of the day. You want me to be the scapegoat!'

'Not at all,' she replied energetically. 'I only want you to follow your conscience when choosing.'

'And I can't say no? Am I allowed to refuse?'

With a smile she said, 'Of course you can refuse but then I'll fight you all the way, even though I don't want to lose a friend.'

He got up. 'Khaled Abdel Rahman,' he said angrily.

She looked at him, she stared at him. He had surprised her.

Hoarsely she asked, 'Will he agree?'

'Does he have a choice? If the head of the department decides to send him to Mozambique, he'll go. And anyway, America is a lovely country. It's an opportunity he wouldn't have dreamed was possible.'

Resonantly she said, 'Then it's a deal.'

Professor Muhammad left. She fell back into her chair. He would leave. Would she make him leave? She? Why? The grant could go to hell. Salma was welcome to it, anyone was! Why had she agreed?

What did she expect? That he would stay with her forever? What did she want?

No. She would not think of what she wanted now. She would not think.

She left her room and headed for the lavatory.

Everything about the English Department was special, particularly the lavatory.

Hanaa's biggest problem with Egypt was lavatories, since they were usually a reflection of a lack of allegiance to authority. They also mirrored the incompetence and carelessness of authority. The lavatories of the English Department, however, were different. They were clean and smelt of flowers, so that the flowers themselves enjoyed being there. There were always paper towels, the lights were always on, the walls white and everything neat and well supervised.

For the past twenty years the department's lavatory had been a shining example of the solidarity of the people and the team effort of the staff members of the department.

The only problem was that the lavatory was for private use only, only for the staff members. It had its own key and no lowly student was allowed to desecrate or defile it.

The students of the English Department, who had long been distinguished from other students by their elegant clothes and luxurious cars, had to use the lavatory in the Philosophy Department or elsewhere.

Professor Hanaa decided that she would change the staff's shameful position on the matter and provide each student of the English Department with a key to the lavatory. She was certain that everyone would praise both her and her achievements. However, she strictly prohibited students from other departments from using the lavatory. To further ensure that only serious English Department students used the lavatory, she issued a decree that the privilege of using the lavatory went only to students from the second year on; in other words, after they had successfully finished their first year. How she wished she could let all the people of Egypt use clean lavatories! If only she were not simply the head of the English Department! Maybe sometime in the future when she had a position of more power and authority, she could be of benefit to everyone.

These were the thoughts going through her head as she made her way to the toilet.

She looked at herself in the mirror, looked at the dark shadows under her eyes, the wrinkles that pulled her cheeks down to her mouth. What did she expect?

She was wearing a black turtleneck, a tartan kilt teamed up with black stockings and shoes with stiletto heels.

She smiled to herself. She was tiny compared to him, even in her stilettos. Only in stature, of course, not in status or anything else ... in that sense, she was a giant! She was everything.

She combed her hair back into a ponytail and applied a bit of eyeliner and lip gloss.

She had a small thin-lipped mouth, and with those very same thin lips she would tell him the wonderful news of her great achievement, one that was no less important than her achievement with the lavatory issue.

She closed her eyes, then left the lavatory and headed for the staff room. The minute she walked in, everyone leapt to their feet out of awe and respect. He was there, too. She did not look at him. She could not.

He made her laugh. He was bursting with vitality; he was strong. Why was she talking about him as if he was over and done with! Then there was the grant ... but she could still go on seeing him for months.

She was still beautiful; she could see the constant admiration in his eyes. She was beautiful, graceful, strong, enchanting! She sat down and looked at Salma, who was wearing a tight short skirt and a short white blouse. She could see her belly button clearly through her shirt. Hanaa scowled. How did her parents allow her to leave the house like that? Loftily she asked, 'How are you all?'

'Fine. Thank you so much. Thank you, professor,' they all replied in unison.

'The trip to Alexandria was lovely,' Muhammad burst out enthusiastically.

Khaled, smiling scornfully, looked at Salma and said, 'Especially the belly-dancing competition.'

Salma frowned and remained silent. 'The faculty excels particularly at belly-dancing,' Khaled went on.

She could sense his unease with Salma. She embodied everything that he hated, the exorbitant richness, the liberalism, the vulgar clothes, everything that he found disgusting.

He did not hide his hatred, and Salma could not understand it!

Rising, Hanaa said, 'Khaled, I want you in my office.'

He nodded in agreement. He seemed tired and agitated. She did not know what was wrong with him.

Putting his hands together in a gesture of surrender he said, 'I'm at your command, professor.'

'What's wrong with you?' she whispered looking at him.

With a strange formality he said, 'I was up all night studying. I didn't sleep well.'

She looked at him once again. She knew he had not been studying. He was working, giving private tutoring all night long, lessons that sometimes started at one o'clock in the morning.

'Khaled', she said forcefully. 'I know everything. I already asked you to stop giving private lessons. If you don't, I'll have you brought up before the disciplinary board.'

He sat down and said coldly, 'If I stop giving private lessons, who'll support me financially? My family? The university? The government? The new world order?

'So you admit it?'

'To you, professor, it's an insignificant matter. But it's my livelihood you're talking about. Never deprive anyone of their livelihood or else—'

'Are you threatening me?'

'Most Egyptians have to grovel in the mire for their livelihood and wouldn't hesitate to kill anyone who deprived them of it ... and since they will kill to survive, they will not be murderers but martyrs. It's a dangerous game you're playing, interfering with people's sustenance in a way I don't understand.'

She burst out vehemently, 'How dare you speak to me like that?! I was going to give you some good news.'

He looked at her in amazement.

'We chose you for the grant to America.'

He looked closely at her, 'Why me?'

Without looking at him she said forcefully, 'Aren't you going to thank me? Khaled, listen. Stop giving lessons. Don't force me to take action against you – you know I will.'

He drew near whispering. 'Listen, Professor Hanaa. Professor Samy just asked me to help him get rid of you and I told him I'd think about it. Don't make it easy. Don't make things work out badly for you.'

She smiled sarcastically, 'You're welcome to him, Khaled. You and he are nothing to me. If you don't stop giving private lessons, I'll bring you up before the board within two weeks. Do you want the grant?'

Getting up he calmly declined. 'No, I don't.'

'So you can focus on private lessons? This meeting is over, Khaled.'

As he opened the door and was getting ready to leave, she said sternly, 'I warned you never to take liberties with me. Remember?'

He left without an answer, closing the door behind him.

She was seething with a kind of rage she had never felt towards anyone before. She was furious, and she feared herself.

She did not call him. He did not call her.

She knew what he wanted. He wanted to rob her of her history and rewrite it. He wanted to take over, but that was impossible.

He no longer liked waiting timidly till she allowed him to see her. No, he no longer relished playing a secondary role in her life. He wanted a lot, and he demanded a lot, but she could no longer give. She had never taken to him. She did not love him. Giving was against her nature. He wanted to force her to be giving ... and that was utterly impossible.

She lay on the bed, yearning for him, hating him, longing for his touch, despising his arrogance and his stubbornness and knowing that this was the end. He had turned down the grant.

There were laws that had to be obeyed; people could not just live as they pleased. There were laws that had been disregarded for years. She represented the law, the government, the state and her institution. She had never wronged her institution, since her allegiance was first and foremost to it.

No, he did not call her, nor did she call him, even though she wanted to clarify things with him one last time so there would be no confusion. She wanted to point out that the agreement had been only a secret marriage. He could break the deal if he wanted to, but what he could not do was challenge her!

She waited a few days, scheming and plotting as to how to teach Khaled a lesson he would never forget.

***

She looked at her sister with a mixture of hesitancy and astonishment.

Her sister was giving a religious lesson. She was calm and confident. Her heavyset body filled the chair and her arms were stretched out before her. She no longer cared about being fat, about dieting, about men. She was a leader, admired by everyone. She kept retelling her tragic story, about how God had saved her and how she got through this fearful tribulation, while the women looked at her, their eyes brimming with tears.

They left after the gathering of the sisterhood apprehensive and respectful.

Leila breathed a sigh of relief then called the porter. Once, twice. When he finally came she neither threatened him nor shouted at him as she used to.

She said forcefully, 'May God forgive you, Abdou. I've been calling you for an hour; my voice is hoarse. May God forgive you.'

As if stung by a poisoned dart, Abdou excused himself fearfully, 'Hajja, I was out buying things. God is my witness. I didn't hear you.'

'God knows whether or not you heard me; may God forgive you.'

Breathing heavily he said, 'Your orders, Hajja.'

She gave her orders, and he responded.

Hanaa looked on in wide-eyed amazement.

Sitting there with her new-found confidence, Leila said, 'How are you, Hanaa? You are lucky to have nothing to do with men and their disgusting ways. You should thank God for that.'

She swallowed. There was a strange sensation in her throat. 'Yes, Leila. Thank God. How are the children?'

'I know nothing about them,' she said indifferently. 'God will compensate me.'

'Leila, Lobna is a good girl.'

'She loves her father and visits him every day. I never get to see her.'

'It's natural for her to love her father.'

'Yes, it's natural.'

'She needs you,' Hanaa whispered.

'I needed her.'

'Sameh needs you even more. I don't like the way he looks.'

'May God forgive them!'

Hanaa left, her feeling of alienation growing daily, her knowledge of Egypt diminishing at the same rate. Literature books dwindled like street urchins, poverty reigned and women looked for their sustenance in various places, always innovating. In a world ruled by men, a woman had to innovate on a daily basis. Now she understood why Scheherazade had made up a new story every day. A Middle Eastern woman is a master of innovation – she can conjure up something new and play a new role each day. Her whole life she is surrounded by men, bound by men, dependent on men. She is at a man's mercy; he can either bring her down or raise her to the loftiest heights and enthrone her by his side. She is under his thumb – a man's thumb! He could either set her free or keep her a prisoner for life. Now religion had become a new weapon for her, a new form of power. It arouses awe in men, sometimes holding them in check, at other times raising a woman to the status of royalty. How wretched was a woman's lot in the midst of poverty, corruption, frustration and fear. How wretched! Hanaa was so fed up with all this that she wished she could sleep in peace, only to awake and find that Scheherazade had stopped telling stories and that women had stopped reinventing themselves every day. And what else?

And life had not passed her by. Men were not in control; history was being written by women who stood tall and confident, neither loving nor giving, nor fearing their treacherous body nor—

She would sleep peacefully, like she used to forty years ago when Khaled had not yet been born. She had willpower, her life was ahead of her, her work was successful and fruitful. She was now in a position of leadership at the university, and leadership and power were enthralling.

Yes! She would think of her accomplishments, her ambitions and her shining future.

She was irritable and impatient these days. Yes, she was far too touchy. All she really needed was a bit of time to plan.

She was fed up with it all and wanted to sleep in peace.

Chapter 7

Hanaa told the cab driver to wait for her to return. She didn't know the way back home out of the alleys of Boulaq, nor did she want to drive her Peugeot through these bad streets.

She asked the cab driver sternly, 'How much will you charge?'

'Whatever you wanna pay, miss.'

How she hated the word 'miss'. She said sharply, 'Tell me, how much?'

'Twenty.'

'What? Do you think I'm a tourist? I'll be back in half an hour. And I won't pay more than ten.'

She didn't give him a chance to speak, and got out of the cab. In disgust, she looked at the building, which almost seemed to be collapsing. Then she started climbing the dark, narrow stairs, on which all kinds of smells lingered, from the stench of urine to the stink of old garlic, onion, cooking and mould.

She placed her hand over her mouth and nose, and rang the doorbell.

His mother opened the door. She scrutinized her for a moment then said, 'Salaam aleikum, my daughter.'

Hanaa smiled and stretched out her hand saying, 'I'm Professor Hanaa. Khaled's supervisor.'

The mother invited her in with warmth. 'Please, come in.'

Hanaa looked around. It was a simple flat, yet extremely clean. What drew her attention most was that all the lamps were glistening, as if calling out to her, 'Our mistress is an excellent housewife. We all love her!'

Shaimaa came out of her room, exclaiming warmly, 'Professor Hanaa! Do you remember me?'

She smiled, shaking hands with Shaimaa, 'Yes, of course I remember you.'

Hanaa shook hands without actually closing her hand around Shaimaa's fingers. She shook hands like a queen who has become bored with handshakes. She gave Shaimaa her hand without exerting any effort to move her fingers and palm.

Shaimaa said hurriedly, 'Khaled isn't here. I'll call him on his mobile phone. He'll come right away.'

She nodded.

Khaled's mother sat down, analysing her for a moment. Then she said, 'You are very young.'

Hanaa smiled, but did not reply.

The mother reaffirmed, 'By God, you certainly are young. And you are the head of the department?'

She nodded.

The mother went on eagerly, 'Khaled works night and day. Khaled has always been bright and successful. You know, when he was little, his father worked at the Ministry of the Interior. He would take Khaled along. Khaled knew the Koran by heart when he was just five. May God keep him safe. He is my solace from God. My only wish is to see him take his PhD.'

Hanaa replied, 'That will be soon, we hope. I know Khaled very well. He deserves all the best. He's very generous.'

His mother pursed her lips and said hurriedly, 'May God bestow His bounty on him ... Generous! Khaled is generosity itself. I just want to see him married.'

Hanaa looked in surprise at his mother, who explained warmly, 'His younger brother is married. I want to see him married, too.'

Hanaa smiled, 'God has the power to grant your very wish.'

'Yes, you're right.'

'Who knows, you may find him married very soon.'

'God willing.'

'Maybe even today.'

The mother was taken aback, but Hanaa laughed and said, 'I have good news for him. Shall I tell you? We chose him for a scholarship.'

Alarmed again, the mother asked, 'Does that mean he'll go abroad? No! No, I don't want him to travel. I mean, if he has to—'

Hanaa was getting impatient with the mother's constant reference to him as if he were a rare plant or a precious diamond, but said, 'Let's wait till he arrives. Is he coming now?'

Shaimaa said hurriedly, 'Five minutes.'

His mother got up and said warmly, 'I'll make you some mango juice.'

She looked around the living room. The pink covers had been carefully washed, the window was wide open, the blue linen curtains were ironed. Poor Khaled! This is what he expected in his wife, then. All this care, and laundry, and ironing, and cooking, and fresh mango juice. Poor Khaled.

She looked around her. This was his home, then. His childhood, his life. It was a small flat, of course. The hall was carefully painted in a cheap simple white. The sun flooded in from all sides, and all the windows were open. The walls were covered in large boards with verses of the Koran, and a picture of his father. The hall also served as the dining room. To the left was the sitting room, separated by glass-panelled doors. She loved those old doors with their two oval-shaped glass panes. Whenever Khaled's mother tried to open the door, the frame creaked with fatigue and age. It was an old door, but she liked it.

The house was extremely humble: clean and confined. She didn't see his room, but could imagine it. A cheap wooden bed and a small desk. No doubt, his mother and sister's room would be crowded with things old and new.

This is you, then, Khaled. You come from this plain little flat full of Koranic verses, full of sunlight streaming through its windows. She listened to the recitation of the Koran drifting over from the kitchen, where Khaled's mother was cooking, and other recitations and the call to prayer floating in through the various windows.

This was Khaled's home, next to the old mosque down the street. Was he happy here? Was he happy now?

She smiled, overcome by a warmth the source of which she couldn't make out. She knew him better now. She understood what he meant when he said he had to hurry to offer the dawn prayer at the mosque. He had always done so, ever since he was a child. Not that the mosque was that far away; it was not far at all. And this street never slept.

She had expected to cringe at the sight of sewage flooding the street, at the dust, the unbearable pollution, the poverty, the squalor, the garbage, the ignorance, the collapsing stairs, the weak nagging women, the coarse men, the fat food, the sweet pastries! But she wasn't cringing. She hadn't cringed at anything.

Why?

She didn't know. She just hadn't.

When he finally walked into the living room, he looked at her and smiled tenderly. Her heart skipped a beat, and she was overwhelmed by a rush of emotions. How she missed his smile, his laughter, his sarcasm ... his everything!

Closing the glass door slowly behind him, he whispered, 'This is a most unexpected surprise, professor. If I were naïve, I'd think you missed me and couldn't bear not seeing me in all this time. Is this why you are here? Did you really miss me?'

She was about to speak, but he hurried on teasingly, 'No, no, don't speak. You'll only say "No" and break my heart as you always do!'

This time she burst out laughing. His mother opened the door and brought in the juice. She said with warmth, 'Khaled, you never told me that Professor Hanaa was so young and beautiful. But she has to eat a bit.'

His eyebrows shot up in surprise, and he looked at Hanaa. Their eyes locked, but he didn't say anything. His mother went out again, closing the door. Silence prevailed for a moment while she sipped her mango juice calmly. Then she said, 'Since I've known you, I've put on ten pounds.'

He smiled and replied, 'Since I've known you, I've understood how Muhammad Ali managed to massacre the Mamluks at the Citadel so calmly and effectively, and then forget all about them.'

There was silence, as if each was trying to read the other's mind. Hanaa spoke first. 'We are so different in everything.'

He answered calmly, 'In a lot of things, but not everything.'

'You prefer a system that is based on corruption. You want Salma and her ilk to take over the whole country.'

'A small degree of corruption is desirable and only human. If we enforced all laws to the letter, we would forget our humanity. Take a traffic light, for example. Doesn't the traffic policeman sometimes allow you to park your car in a no-parking zone in return for a small tip? There is nothing wrong there: that tip may feed him and his family. And you may be too exhausted to walk, or have your kids with you. He scratched your back, and you scratched his. It's none of the government's business. How often do people drive around without their licence? If every time you were stopped because you were driving without a licence and taken to the station, the country would come to a standstill. If I didn't have connections to help me get my ID, I would be held at the police station every day of my life. Connections help a lot.'

'You're in defence of corruption. Why?'

'Because I'm an Egyptian, and there is no Egyptian who has not given in to corruption. There is no Egyptian who hasn't invited some important person for lunch, or hasn't licked the boots of his superiors, or hasn't slipped a policeman a pound. This is our way of life, professor.'

'Then you'll become corrupt. You'll give Salma and the likes of her better chances.'

'At times we need to make sacrifices. But I'll never lose my humanity. Being human is more important than justice.'

'You are weird. At times I feel like we're worlds apart. Are we from the same country?'

'I don't know. Where are you from?'

'Where are *you* from?'

'Egypt is a vast country, professor. It can hold us all.'

She considered for a moment, then she asked with a touch of regret in her voice, 'Why did you turn down the scholarship?'

He looked at her and explained, 'I can't leave my family. I'm their only source of income.'

Feeling a pang of jealousy, she probed further, 'But what about your future? You have to think of that, too.'

He nodded and said, 'Yes, my future. Which reminds me that I'm married. Or quasi-married.'

She whispered longingly, 'Khaled.'

He answered coldly, 'Yes, professor?'

'Take the scholarship.'

He stared at her, and said with a mixture of surprise and anger, 'To get rid of me? Or to make me rise to your academic and scholarly standard? Or to make me learn democracy as you master it?'

'Why are you so cruel?' she asked in surprise.

He suddenly burst out, 'Because I'm fed up with this way of life. Either you declare our marriage publicly or we go our separate ways.'

She asked quietly, 'And when I declare our marriage, do you think it will work out?'

'Do you want it to work out?'

'Do you?'

Khaled said quickly, 'Stop answering my questions with questions! Do you want it to work out?'

'It won't. It cannot. And you know all the reasons,' Hanaa replied.

He answered with fervour, 'Never say never. No differences or pressures ever stopped me. I always get what I want.'

'Ask yourself what you want first, then, before you take any decisions.'

Following a sudden inspiration, he suggested, 'Muhammad deserves this scholarship!'

'That's your humane side speaking now.'

'Muhammad deserves it, professor. But I know you will be forced to grant it to Salma. My humble advice is to give it to Salma to save your neck from the Dean. If you want to keep your post, that is.'

He turned his face away, so as not to hug her. He didn't speak.

She walked calmly over to him, whispering as she approached, 'You constantly challenge me. Our relationship is complicated and strange. Sometimes I feel guilty towards you. Sometimes I fear you. Most of the time I think of you.'

He turned his face away from her.

She whispered with a touch of pain in her voice, 'You're dejected because you sense the end is near.'

He said confidently, 'There will be no end. Give up the chairmanship so that I can deal with you. Stop supervising my dissertation and see me like a woman sees a man.'

She sighed and whispered again, 'You want to break me. Why? So that I look up to you in submission like your mother and sister do? To wash your clothes and make you tea? You know I won't do that.'

'I just want you to be my wife. I don't care if you make me tea or not. I want you beside me, not above me.'

'I'm sorry, Khaled. I can't. I was born to lead, not to eat pastries, or to give and love and hate too much.'

'You're the worst leader I've ever seen. You're too straight, too honest, too tyrannical even as you seek justice. They're all serious deficiencies that will lead you to collapse. You're not devious or docile, but you don't listen to anyone ... and you love a challenge.'

She glared, enraged. 'You simply can't give up your Middle Eastern mentality. You can't stand seeing me successful.'

Before he could say anything, she asked defiantly, 'Khaled, you want me to declare our marriage, don't you?'

He answered drily, 'No. Of course not. You can't possibly declare your marriage to a man with a Middle Eastern mentality.'

She glared at him angrily and defiantly, then stormed out of the room, heading for the hall, towards the front door. He came in tow and opened the door for her, his face distorted with anger. Khaled's mother called after her respectfully and invitingly, 'professor, won't you have something else to drink? Why don't you have lunch with us?'

She smiled wryly and looked at his sister sitting in the hall, then his mother. She walked over to his mother, kissed her cheek and said, 'Maybe next time. Bye for now, my mother-in-law.'

Then, walking out, she hissed at Khaled, 'Good luck. My heart goes out to you. I just declared our marriage! Don't you dare say a word!'

She closed the door and a dead silence descended upon the place. The sound of the closing door reverberated in him as if his heart were hollowed out, and he mumbled, 'You fucking bitch!'

His mother fell onto a chair, hesitantly asking her daughter, 'Shaimaa ... is that woman off her rocker?'

He swallowed hard and turned to face his mother, but didn't utter a word.

His mother stammered, 'Khaled, she just said you were her husband. Did you hear that? Did she say that, Shaimaa?'

Shaimaa said heatedly, 'Yes. I heard her.'

His mother asked feebly, 'Has she gone mad, or what?'

Calmly walking towards his room, he said, 'She's my wife. Yes. She's my wife.'

He closed his eyes, and tried to place his hands over his ears, fully aware of what was about to happen. Of course he knew what was about to happen.

He heard his mother's scream, followed by Shaimaa yelling, 'Mum, Mum. Can you hear me? Mum, I'll phone Abdallah.'

His sister opened the door while he silently tried to come to grips with what had happened. How was he to explain everything to them? How would they take it? For the first time he was going to stand accused. He would be exposed to the worst forms of psychological and emotional harassment. His sister would take the lead to avenge herself of him and to challenge his authority. He was trapped by the wishes and desires of all those around him, by all their opinions. His mother would feel lost – because she had lost him, because he had stabbed her in the back. Because, because, because ...

Professor Hanaa had dealt him the death blow.

And the professor believed that women in Egypt were deprived of their rights! What about men? The torture and all the worst forms of psychological subjugation that he was now exposed to? The pressure, the threats, the blame, the responsibility!

He covered his face for a moment, then got up slowly to go to his mother. She was on her bed in her room weeping, as if her son had just died.

As soon as she saw him, her weeping became a wailing, and she yelled, 'Why did you have to do that to your mother, Khaled? You of all people? Why, son? Why did you allow Satan into our home and bring your mother's wrath upon you? You, Khaled, of all people?'

He could have tried to convince her that getting married was not something to bring on God's wrath and that he had not intended to hurt her. But he knew she would not understand. She felt that he had hurt her deeply. Much deeper than if she had found out her husband had married someone else in secret.

He took her hand and kissed it, whispering, 'I'm sorry. It couldn't be helped.'

Crying, and wiping her tears, she said, 'I'll never forgive you, until you divorce her. Divorce her, son. May God lead you back to the right path.'

Once again he could have asked why. He knew the answer, though. Because she was older. Because she was a loose woman. Because she moved in different circles. Because, because, because ...

Why not? She didn't want him any more! Why should he fight for a woman who did not fight for him? Why?

He was not used to defeat. He was not used to weakness. He was not used to needing a woman this badly.

It might be for the best if he divorced her and married Safaa or any other girl. He would work, have children and—

He wanted a submissive wife, not one who constantly defied him. And she certainly should not have a mind of her own with firm convictions that could not be changed! Never. There was nothing more ugly than a woman with an aim and a mind of her own. Such a woman could cut a man up like a chainsaw. No, he didn't want an independent mind.

His mother said again, 'Divorce her, if you want me to forgive you before I die!'

Involuntarily he answered, 'I can't.'

'You're infatuated with her like a teenager! I thought I had brought a man into the world! A man, not a weakling! What's come over you? Has she put a spell on you? Oh my goodness! She has neither looks nor beauty. What could you possibly love about her? What's gotten into you, son? What a loss! Oh God, let me die before I see my son drooling over a woman like that one.'

He didn't speak. He walked to his room in silence, stopped at the door and whispered, 'Calm down, Mum.'

As soon as he had left the room, she turned to his sister, wailing, 'Oh my, oh my. Shaimaa, did you see the dazed look in his eyes? She's bewitched him! Let's go to your aunt, my daughter. We have to find a solution for this. He has a family, he has folks who can stand up for him. And this witchcraft has to be reversed before she drags him down like a dog! Oh what a loss!'

Khaled's mother said beseechingly, 'Muhammad, my son, may God protect you. Please tell him – he's your friend. We're at a loss with him. He won't listen to anyone.'

'Don't you worry, Hajja. I will, God willing, talk him out of it.'

Muhammad went into Khaled's room, and told him as if he could see him, 'Why, look how pale you are. No doubt your mum won't cook for you after this heavy blow you dealt her.'

Khaled smiled, but kept silent.

'You go get married, you nitwit, and then you tell your mum?'

'She told her,' Khaled answered angrily.

'She? Professor Hanaa?'

Muhammad burst out laughing and said, 'She? Why? Does she hate you that much?'

'The wickedness of women is deadlier than any man's. I would tear her to pieces if I could. Slap her left and right. Muhammad—'

There was a moment of silence, then Muhammad said, 'You still want her.'

'And I'll never leave her.'

'You're being stubborn.'

'Maybe.'

'Why?'

'I don't know.'

'Do you love her that much?'

He closed his eyes, then asked, 'Do you think it's time to get rid of the head of the department?'

Muhammad shouted in alarm, 'Don't you dare, Khaled. She'd never ever forgive you.'

He did not utter a word.

'Khaled, what are you thinking? Khaled?'

'Yes?'

'I'm worried about you. What are you going to do? Why don't you just forget about Professor Hanaa? It's what your mother wants, it's what Professor Hanaa wants, it's what everyone wants. Forget her, then marry Safaa as you had intended, or anyone else.'

He still didn't reply.

'Khaled, why won't you say something? Why would you stand up to the world for a woman who does not want you?'

Khaled still did not answer.

'Will you leave her?'

He suddenly said, 'I have a lot of work to do today. A lot. I'm getting fed up with private tutoring, compliments, smiles, pressure from everyone, everything. I wonder when all this will come to an end.'

'So you're exhausted?'

'My mother won't speak to me. She's pressurizing me to death. My sister is taking revenge. Did I ever hurt my sister? I worried about her. I wanted her to be the best girl in the world. My brother fears the flow of gifts and financial aid for him and his fiancée will dry up. The professor has decided she wants to keep her post and fears for it. And I'm stuck in the middle of all of it. What would you do if you were in my shoes?'

'Go find a hooker and drown my sorrows.'

'Muhammad!'

'Just kidding. You haven't told me yet what Professor Hanaa looks like. Is she beautiful? And don't say maybe!'

The memories were eerie and funny. All he could remember were their moments of intimacy, which were tense and fast: moments when they laughed together, moments when she talked incessantly until he had to leave. He remembered her words, their chats together when he was the patient listener. He remembered how she would raise her eyebrows when she was telling an exciting story. He remembered her thick eyebrows and her delicate glasses. He remembered how she buried her head in the pillow after they had made love, as if bashful or ashamed of herself and her weakness and fear. He sensed how burdened she was by internal conflicts and stress. She always buried her head in her pillow and opened her palm as if expecting him to take her hand. He always gave her his palm and closed his hand over hers for a few minutes without a word. He didn't know if she felt guilty because of this strange marriage. Did she feel bad because she had given herself to him, because she surrendered to her feelings, or because she loved him as a violent but delicate and fearful tyrant? Or did she sense that their relationship was coming to an end but preferred not to see it?

He would remember these moments and resume his monotonous life.

His mother, on the other hand, had pledged to retrieve her son. She used every legitimate and every illegal weapon in her arsenal to do it. Even her strong hatred of Safaa changed into overwhelming love. She would call Safaa daily, flattering her, courting her, as if she herself were the one intending to marry her. He expected Safaa to call him, to try to see him. He felt very nervous these days. He didn't want to hurt Safaa, nor did he want to surrender to the ending his mother, sister and Professor Hanaa had chosen. After all, he was a Middle Eastern man, as Professor Hanaa had put it.

He was a Middle Eastern man, whose history was written for him by another, whose future was written for him by another, whose defeat was dictated to him by another, as were his feelings: tyranny, duplicity and anxiety.

He had to consult with those around him.

He had to trust the women in his life to handle it as they pleased, and trust the men in his life to ruin it as they saw fit.

So he was a Middle Eastern man.

This is what she had said.

He had expected his wife to serve him, while he would serve everyone.

He smiled despairingly. She wanted to throw him in the dustbin now. Professor Hanaa. She was naïve. And her naivety was pathetic, ridiculous, infuriating.

He heard his mobile phone ringing. He looked at the number and knew it was Safaa. He didn't answer, but instead switched off the phone and went to sleep, awaiting the morning.

He smiled sorrowfully, taking a few papers out of his old desk, and then went to the door, to go to his first private lesson for the day.

Memories of nights spent with her dominated his mind. What he truly missed, despite his anger, was their moments of ecstasy when she was in his arms. In those moments, she was like a bird that had lost its feathers in a storm, and the feathers had scattered all over the place.

As for Professor Hanaa – she would be gathering her scattered thoughts, breathing slowly, whispering, 'Khaled. What are you doing to me?'

And every time he'd whisper, 'What is it I'm doing to you?'

'I don't know.'

But he knew. In her voice he detected surrender, the inability to think straight, objection and defiance.

From one moment to the next, she became a woman in his grip. It was only during those brief moments that he could be the ruler, the master, the tyrant!

She gave him these moments peacefully, and these were the moments he now missed.

When she let go of her body, let it tremble and throb with life, she was his woman – only his. At all other times he would see Professor Hanaa surrounded by a throng of men for whom she decided everything. She spoke with confidence, defining all aspects of her life and of her relationships.

Men were usually apprehensive or uncomfortable in her presence. Her dominant personality would shine through her sharp eyes, her confident words, her firm tone.

She did not fear men. She did not fear women. She did not fear anything!

From what he had heard of her family, it would seem to him that she was extremely spoilt. Her birth had been unintended by her elderly parents, and hence there was a ten-year gap between her and her siblings. It seemed to him that her mother had been an extremely strict and aristocratic lady, who held customs and traditions and a woman's duty towards her children in high esteem. Her father had been tender, had smothered her with love and encouraged her, imbuing her with confidence and ambition.

Her father was his problem! Her father was the cause for all this confusion Professor Hanaa lived in.

What was he to do with her?

Should he expose her, divorce her and ruin her?

She deserved that, if not worse!

She thought she was able to get rid of him as she had got rid of her virginity. With the same nonchalance and without a second thought.

What did he want, then?

To see her crushed in front of his eyes. To have her kneel in front of him begging for forgiveness! To watch her beseeching him in fear, yearning for him longingly.

He would not surrender to her rule.

She wanted to ignore him.

Fine. Let her ignore him. He would ignore her too! He would be patient. He had always been. He would be patient and wait until she returned, humiliated and conquered. Maybe he had to work in silence to achieve this goal.

And the directorship of the department? He decided to think calmly. There was a lot he could do.

He had always been patient. He would not act recklessly or stupidly.

There are many things a woman can do to forget a man.

Well, perhaps she missed him at times. But then she had lived a lifetime without him; she would be able to live another one too.

She needed a cat, a good book, classical music and a powerful computer.

She already had the music, the computer and the book. So she needed to get a cat.

She bought a big fat cat, which she spoilt like her own child. She would talk to her, and was happy if she slept with her on her bed.

Her life returned to its previous monotony. The yoghurt, the whole-grain bread, the salads, the jogging, the workouts, the boredom, the loneliness, the long days.

She caught up on her reading and her research, and went back to sitting at her desk for hours analysing words, citing scholars' texts and theories. It was a life deprived of all love, grief and fear.

Once more she focused on one thing, counted on only one thing: herself. She went back to concentrating on herself, to relying on herself. Yet there was a new feeling that seeped into her, made her tingle, dripped through her throat like a cold drop of water. It brought her back to consciousness, but it scared her and drowned her, too. She did not know exactly what that feeling was.

She was happy because the relationship had been terminated. She would not ask him for a divorce. He would give her one in due course; she was certain of that. When she saw him at university, she would see him as one of her students, no more. She would expect him to show allegiance and obedience, no more.

The strange new feeling kept seeping into her veins as cold as ice, but it was totally unfamiliar to her. She tried in vain to identify it, to find it in the novels she taught. She feared Khaled, yet loved him, too. Similarly, she feared this feeling, yet somehow liked it. Was it wrath? Rage? It was overwhelming and slow. Surrender? Longing? Fear? Grief? All the same.

She had called her cat Basbousa.

* * *

Leila, too, was still writing her own history, now that her destiny was in her own hands. Religion had become her sole preoccupation, and her days were busy with events: meetings with the sisters, going to the mosque, charity work, counselling, and providing *fatwa*s. One Saturday, as she was sitting in her room holding a religious book and awaiting the dawn prayers, she felt the door opening slowly.

She had been thinking about Hanaa and what she was going through. She knew the weakness of a woman when her nature took control of her. She was beginning to become suspicious of the relationship between Hanaa and Khaled.

God forbid! May God guide Hanaa to the righteous path!

She felt the door opening slowly, but she did not wish to see any of her children. The odd thing about their household was that she avoided seeing her children, so as not to be reminded of their shame, their weakness, their many sins against her. She prayed to God that whoever was opening the door was not one of them.

It was her son, Sameh. She did not look him in the face. She had not looked at him for months, ever since he had deserted her like a bag of potatoes at her sister's and had not once asked about her.

She wasn't going to look at him now.

She said drily, squatting on her prayer mat, 'What do you want? Money? Go ask your father for some. I have none.'

He sat down on the bed, and said calmly, 'Mum, look at me!'

She averted her face.

He shouted nervously, 'Look at me!'

She trembled briefly, closed her eyes in pain and then said, 'Don't make me angrier at you than I already am. Get out, Sameh!'

He said hysterically, trembling, 'Look at me. Stop what you're doing and look at me. Look at me!'

She mumbled calmly, then said, 'God forgive us, "Thou shalt not chide thy parents", remember – "shalt not chide them"'.

Hysterically he said again, 'Look at me! Look at me, Hajja!'

She turned towards to him, and their eyes locked. But she did not see her son. What she saw was a ghost.

This was not her son.

He had dark rings under his eyes, and his body was gaunt and weakened, as if he had spent years in detention and had not been released yet.

She felt a sharp stab of pain, the like of which she had never felt before. It was a new kind of pain, different from any others that she had experienced. It was not a feeling of impotence or of defeat this time. It was a new feeling very difficult to describe, a feeling of disgrace, of shame, of death.

This defeat was more devastating than all others. Even for her, who suffered a defeat every day!

Bursting into desperate tears, Sameh sobbed, 'I'm dying, Mum. Yesterday, I went into a coma for an hour! I took an overdose. I've been expelled from university. I'm dying, it's over. Can you see your son dying and sit there on your prayer mat?'

She saw his tears on the floor. She saw his tears in front of him. Feelings of anger and defeat, of guilt and grief took control of her.

She raised herself up from the prayer mat, sat down on the bed beside him and whispered, 'Since when?'

He shouted, 'Since when? Now you're asking since when? For a long, long time. Two, three years, who knows?'

Becoming hysterical, she cried, 'Sameh! No, Sameh. You will live, my son. You'll be treated.'

He sat there in apathy, 'I don't know if I even want to be!'

She mumbled while her tears gushed forth, 'Oh please God, please dear God, not my son. Not my son. Please dear God.'

She got up resolutely, and said hoarsely, 'We'll go to hospital now. Now.'

He replied like a child, with a touch of jealousy, 'And the sisterhood, and your meetings? And your charity work?'

'Let's go now. And shut up; don't say a word. God is with us. God knows.'

She moved quickly, shrouding herself in a black robe. She grabbed his hand and pulled him along, saying, 'Now, now.'

'Why? Why now?'

She murmured desperately and hysterically, 'Please dear God, not my son.'

With all her strength she pushed him out of the room, grabbed his hand forcefully and dragged him out of the house and into her car.

* * *

Days later, when Hanaa found out that her nephew was being treated at a rehabilitation facility, she sighed in relief. Coldness was tingling in her throat. Her beautiful cat was asleep in her arms, but the tears wouldn't flow.

The war was erupting around her, but she did not fear wars. On the contrary, she expected them and at times even sought them.

She knew who her enemies were. She was on her guard with everyone, especially Khaled. But she was also certain he would not dare to harm her or announce their marriage, even though his mother knew. No one would know. It was a tacit agreement that Khaled would keep silent. If he spoke, she would destroy him. She was capable of that. Of course this work was his livelihood and he would not – could not – speak out.

She was not ready for today's meeting, and she had not slept well.

It was not an easy meeting. She spoke of the departmental achievements, of how she had managed to increase the budget of the department for the current year more than in all previous years. She spoke of how she had tried to send more than one Teaching Assistant on a scholarship abroad, how the balance had been re-established and how the institution had gained the upper hand over the individual. She spoke of how all had to work in the service of the country, the government and the institution.

Professor Maysah opened her mouth to speak, but Hanaa motioned her to remain silent, resuming proudly, 'I've achieved a lot, and will achieve more. Our most important objective is scientific research.'

Samy smiled sarcastically, but did not say anything.

Maysah said enraged, 'And what about delegations abroad? You can't keep this stupid regulation. It's against university rules.'

Hanaa was infuriated; nothing annoyed her more than someone opposing her or defying her in public. 'No delegations. Not this year, nor next year. We need every professor and researcher,' she ordered.

Khaled sat at the end of the room, and did not look at her. Anger flared in his eyes.

She said forcefully, 'I request you to focus on our work. Let's not create problems. There are regulations that have to be abided by.'

Samy smiled sardonically. 'And you are the one who sets the regulations? There is a dean and a president, and what you are saying is nonsense.'

She started, amidst the murmuring of all those present.

Her reaction drew Khaled's attention. He smiled, looking at her, anticipating her reaction, expecting it!

She shouted forcefully, 'Professor Samy, this is a meeting, not a market place! Please leave the room quietly!'

The people present tried to calm Samy down. Furious, Maysah objected, 'Hanaa, you can't do this. We don't agree.'

'I didn't ask your opinions. I'm the head of the department! I decide. I've been appointed in this post to take decisions by myself.'

Maysah said defiantly, eyeing Hanaa as a woman, not as a professor, 'Everyone has a superior!'

In a challenging tone, Hanaa replied, waving her hand dismissively, 'Go and complain if you want. That's the last I have to say on this topic.'

Silence fell for a moment. Maysah had grabbed her mobile phone and was nervously drumming it on the table. There was no sound but the sound of Maysah hitting the table tensely with her mobile phone, as if she were imagining it to be Hanaa.

Then Hanaa said firmly, 'Stop it, Maysah. You'll break the battery! I'm sure it's already broken, and that looks like a very expensive phone.'

He could see that her blush was deepening as she went on. 'I thought you were going to congratulate me on my ceaseless efforts and on everything I've done for this department. I had not expected this amount of ingratitude!'

Getting up, Maysah said, 'It is God who grants us our livelihoods, Hanaa!'

Then she stormed out, leaving the door open. Samy followed her.

It was a tough meeting. She tried her best to seem relaxed for the remaining part of it, but her mind was searching for a way to punish Samy and Maysah. She would refer them to the disciplinary board. Yes. Then what? She had to talk to the Dean. And this scholarship issue. She had to think calmly. But she also needed help.

When the meeting was over, she said assertively, 'Khaled, I need you.'

He stopped in his tracks, then looked at her coldly.

She was kneading her fingers, as she often did these days. Maysah and Samy's words were still ringing in her ears. She felt an immense wave of danger approaching her. He waited quietly. It was the first time she had seen him face to face in two months. She avoided his eyes, and focused on his protruding Adam's apple and his chequered shirt. In a monotone, she asked, 'Did you see those fools?'

He looked at her face, but she avoided his eyes again. Scrutinizing her expression, he said indifferently, 'You look tired.'

In a sarcastic tone she asked, 'Are you worried about me? You know I need your help.'

He whispered challengingly, 'Do you, professor?'

She answered instantly, 'Yes.'

He smiled and said, 'Give me one reason why I should help you.'

She replied nervously, 'You give me one reason why you shouldn't. Did I ever wrong you? Did I ever mistreat you? Did I ever use you?'

He smiled, 'Never. You were the best of wives.'

She shouted in panic, 'Don't you dare utter that word, Khaled! It's all over.'

'All right, then. Since all is over, may I leave?'

'Will you help me?'

'Help yourself, professor.'

She answered disdainfully, 'You'll take their side? The side of corruption, bribery and deceit? Fine. You're a nobody anyway.'

He opened the door, anger etched in his every feature. He left the office with an overwhelming desire to slap her face and shake her forcefully.

She would go to see the Dean. She would not keep still. She would attack them before they attacked her.

She would tell him about her achievements and successes. About Maysah's envy, Samy's hatred, the Teaching Assistants' resentment and the general desire to commercialize education and scholarship.

The Dean would understand and appreciate her loyalty and efforts, her continuous work and her love for Egypt, for the government, for the university and all the state's institutions. He would approve of her wish to work through the institution and not through any other extra-institutional structure – none of those networks of individuals connected by poverty, religion, despair, love or hatred. She would work for the sake of Egypt.

She would tell him about what she had achieved and what she planned to achieve. He would be proud of her feats, of her vigilant conscience, of her bright mind. She would be a glorious role model for Egyptian women, as someone who had sacrificed everything for the sake of knowledge, even her personal happiness.

In the presence of the Dean she started speaking with confidence and enthusiasm, with anger and defiance.

He listened patiently and earnestly. When she had finished, she added heatedly, 'Samy must be referred to the board. He was terribly rude to me during a public meeting, just because I'm a woman. I want him to be referred to the disciplinary board. He and Maysah.'

The Dean looked at her, resting his head in his palm. Then he said, 'You've a black heart, Hanaa.'

She answered excitedly, 'He started it. He did. I'm simply enforcing the law. Those who err have to be punished. I want all teaching assistants who are engaged in private tutoring to be questioned. I don't have any concrete evidence yet, but when I do find it, I will immediately start with the investigation, even if I have to question the whole department. You do of course understand the importance of scientific research, and the necessity of a respectful attitude towards one's university. We have teaching assistants and assistant lecturers in their forties who have not finished their PhDs yet because they constantly give private lessons. I want to have them transferred to administrative jobs. We cannot keep providing them with opportunities they do not deserve when there are young people keen on serving the university who do deserve them. This is all because of private tutoring and a lack of allegiance to the university!'

He nodded and resigned himself to agreeing with her. 'Ok, Hanaa. Have it your way.'

She had not expected such a fast victory. She looked at him, studied him, then confirmed, 'All my way?'

He replied enthusiastically, 'I support you fully, Hanaa. And I appreciate your efforts and your relentless work. I will even give you a pay rise.'

She scrutinized him again, her eyes keeping contact with his. He smiled and added, 'You know, I have a personal remark for you.'

She remained confident, 'Please go ahead, professor.'

'In Egypt, people don't keep eye contact when they discuss something. It's considered rude, you see? I mean, in the United

States you can look the speaker straight in the eye, but not here in Egypt. You always fix me with your eyes like that, which is very disconcerting.'

Trying to salvage the situation, she answered hurriedly, 'Yes, of course. I didn't mean any offence.'

He mumbled, 'There is a reason for every spinster in Egypt!'

She asked eagerly, 'Do you approve the investigation?'

'Yes. The investigation, the ban on private tutoring and your way of running things.'

She smiled victoriously. Getting up, she said, 'Thank you for your time, professor.'

He went on nonchalantly, 'Do sign Salma's papers. She deserves this scholarship.'

She smiled bitterly. How naïve she had been!

She answered calmly, 'But the department does not approve. All the professors nominated someone else.'

'But I want her to go.'

'But—'

He interrupted her sharply, 'I don't have the time for all this, Hanaa. I've been listening to you for an hour. Sign Salma's papers first.'

She asked flatly, 'And if I don't? Will you dismiss me from my post?'

He stared at her as if she had accused him of killing the leadership, entering an alliance with the enemy and rigging the polls.

'No, of course I won't dismiss you. I appointed you, because I trust you. Of course I won't dismiss you! But I will leave you to solve your problems with your department on your own. I won't intercede. If you're eliciting my help, you have to act sensibly with these situations. OK?'

She answered, as if summarizing his words, 'If I refuse to grant Salma the scholarship, you will leave me alone to wage war with them. I will have to fight using my own claws, without expecting help from you. But you won't dismiss me. If I agree to the scholarship, you will back me.'

'To the bitter end. And you'll run this department for the rest of your life.'

She answered swiftly, 'Give me a chance to think this over.'

'You know what you want.'

'I think so. But I need time. A day or two, no more.'

She left, knowing exactly what she wanted.

Of course she could grant Salma the scholarship. But she was also capable of battling with them on her own. She would think it over carefully. The way to fight them.

No. She was not going to grant Salma the scholarship! Over her dead body. The day her allegiance went to the Dean, to favouritism, to flattery, that day her academic conscience would die.

* * *

Her days were long and monotonous. The feeling of a void inside her, and of the numbness in her limbs, grew day by day.

She took hold of her hair, remembering her mother, who had been extremely strict. She would divide Hanaa's hair in three parts and would then plait it forcefully, as if trying to tear it out from its roots. When Hanaa complained, or grumbled, or said pleadingly, 'Mum, please, it hurts', her mother would reprimand her with finality. 'You'll get used to the pain.'

You'll get used to the pain.

In not much time, she did get used to it. Her hair, so tightly pulled back, felt as if it was meant to be like that naturally. At times she would specifically ask her mother to pull it back tightly. She was used to the feeling of her hair being pulled out of her skull, every day, for years past!

What was it then?

Just a feeling of discomfort, nothing else.

She lay down on her bed to think. What next? What was she working towards? She would end up in her sixties all alone in this house. She would write her history, but nobody would read it. She would die, but nobody would remember her. How she missed him! She had been brainless that day when she allowed the woman in her to take over and strip her of everything. She had been brainless that day when she lusted for him like a temptress or an enchantress. She had been brainless that day when she gave way and let the woman inside her roar and stir forth.

Fine. That was the end. Fine. She would move on with her life. She would forget him in a year, or two, or three. She would forget him.

She petted her cat, while a strange sense of pain seeped into her gut, growing stronger and spreading.

She knew it was the pain of that void inside her. As it became worse and worse, and she felt the blood erupting inside her, she grabbed the phone – but didn't know who to call.

She screamed, holding her stomach.

Who was she to call?

If she were to die now, who was she to call?

Who would discover her death?

She screamed again, slowly crawling to the door to summon the doorman. She couldn't stand up. Panting, she dropped to the floor, and then didn't feel anything any more. Nothing.

Chapter 8

Endometriosis. That was what they called it. She did not know what it meant. Right now she could not speak. Her eyes spotted ghosts around her. Her tongue was dry and her heart seemed to beat with difficulty. She no longer wrote her own history; it was fate which wrote it. Maybe she was pregnant? She didn't ask, nor did she want to know.

To save her, they had to resort to a hysterectomy. She didn't ask or question.

Her body was in the hands of strangers, and she wasn't able to control anything at all. What really got to her was the feeling that so many people were in control of her at this moment; so many ruled over her. It was the feeling of her physical weakness. It was huge and gruesome.

What frightened her was the fact that she was a woman, and a part of her femininity was being literally excised without her consent. She had been reduced to a mere body lying on a narrow bed. Extremely narrow. An emaciated body, fatigued by the long road. She was just a body on a bed without any privacy.

Everything in the ward was impersonal. The bed. The sheets. The body. The faces. Nobody loved or hated her. She was nobody.

She was just a body on a bed, nothing more.

She was not Professor Hanaa – or even Hanaa.

She was a woman on white sheets and a narrow bed, bleeding to death. A woman like Khaled's mother, Shaimaa, Safaa, Leila, Lobna, Maysah and so many others.

Beneath her were white sheets. Above her white sheets. A woman, no more.

When she was in his arms, she was a woman, no more.

When she yearned for him, she was a woman, no more.

When she turned forty, she was a woman, no more.

When she lost her virginity, she was a woman, no more.

Her weakness was driving her into an abyss. Her body was pushing her into death, blood, demise.

She felt a hand patting her cheek tenderly. A doctor's hand. She opened her eyes. Neutrally, indifferently, he asked, 'Are you OK?'

She nodded.

In the same neutral voice he asked, 'Who can we call? Your husband? Your family?'

She answered in a weakened but determined voice, 'No. Don't call anyone. I'm OK, am I not?'

Slightly taken aback he replied, 'Yes, but you have to stay here. A couple of weeks at least. Are you sure? You don't want me to phone someone?'

She answered in the same tone, 'No.'

Indifferently he asked, 'And are you paying the hospital bill? The doorman called the ambulance. Are the bills charged to your name?'

Pain was resurfacing. 'Yes.'

He patted her shoulder and said, 'Get some rest now. The nurse will get you a sedative. The pain may be severe at first. This was no minor operation. But you're OK, you're a strong woman.'

In a few days, or weeks perhaps, she would go back home, but a part of her was gone forever. She would return to the dark room, the sound of water dripping in the bathroom, monotonous and boring.

She would return to the old kitchen where the shadows of history, death and loneliness lingered, to the tall window and to the tunes drifting in from outside, scattering around her. They were sad and gloomy tunes.

She would return to battling with her brother, demanding her mother's gold. She would return again to the long nights, the grand comfortable bed and the sweeping success which crushed everything.

She closed her eyes.

Excruciating pain was raging in her abdomen.

She didn't want to see anyone. She wouldn't tell anyone. She didn't want those looks of pity, of gloating, of weakness, of—

She sighed, and felt the door opening slowly. Her eyes were closed, but she knew it was him. She had sensed him, and knew he would come.

She kneaded her fingers nervously as she always did when she was tense. Then she opened her eyes slowly as she called out for him. 'Khaled!'

He smiled. She did not know what to make of that smile. Was it pity? Gloating? Shame? Sorrow? She didn't know.

She said with a tinge of bitterness and sarcasm, 'I'm paying for wronging you, then, Khaled. This is my punishment. Do I confess to all my sins now and beg for forgiveness?'

He sat down on the chair next to her bed, and his fingers started impulsively to draw circles on her arm around the extending tubes. He whispered, 'All your sins. Ask for forgiveness for every sin. All of them. Of course I'm only here to gloat. To see you begging for forgiveness. Oh, Professor Hanaa? Why do you do this to me?'

Despite her pain, she answered vehemently, 'I'm sick and tired of you and your shackles, your quarrels and arrogance.'

He answered sharply, 'Look who's talking about haughtiness! Professor, the word "haughty" was coined to describe you.'

She said bitterly, 'Go, Khaled. I don't want to see you now. I think we'll get a quiet divorce, with no further hassle.'

He stood up calmly.

She had not expected that. He turned his face away, then opened the window. He shoved his hands into his pockets and looked out of the window.

Then he echoed, 'A quiet divorce, with no further hassle.'

She could only see his back, and didn't know what he was feeling. She would have paid her life to know what he felt now. An overwhelming curiosity took over.

There was silence for a moment, then she asked challengingly, 'Do you love me?'

Focusing his eyes on the dark light shaft, he replied quietly 'I adore you.'

She closed her eyes again, feeling the tears welling up, but not falling. They never fell.

He didn't utter a word. Nor did she.

Then she said nervously, 'I don't want you to see me like this. Please leave.'

He was still staring out into the dark light shaft when he had noticed a small mouse playing in the rubbish. It leaped across, then disappeared, only to appear again: life among the rubbish. Then it vanished, and he awaited its return with a sudden sense of longing, as if the mouse had become a symbol of life amidst the waste and the darkness.

How could the mouse survive among the decay and dirt, the old wall, the garbage tumbling down on him from every corner? If the decay did not suffocate it, if it was used to the decay and the rotten smell of death, how could it survive in the darkness and among the heavy stones, and in spite of everyone's wish to get rid of it? Its food might be poisoned, or it could be part of a trap the mouse couldn't discern in the dark, a trap he would see only when it was too late.

Poor mouse. It wouldn't live for long. It was bound to die and rot away, too and become itself part of the waste and the darkness in the light shaft.

He said quietly, 'I'm not looking at you, professor, and I don't want to look at you.'

She answered anxiously, 'Just go.'

He was waiting for the mouse to come. He was hoping it would come. He sensed a movement. There it was, buried in the garbage, moving confidently and purposefully, as if it did not care for all this, nor feel any of it. It was small and naïve and had an amazing power to survive. Whenever the mouse hopped into his eyeline, he felt a great sense of relief.

He did not answer.

Nor did she repeat her request to him to leave.

A few minutes later she pushed the call button, as if she had forgotten his presence, and awaited the nurse. The nurse came in, but Khaled never moved or spoke.

She said in the commandeering tone she still mastered, 'I want to use the bathroom. Help me up.'

The nurse smiled sullenly, and held out her arm to help her get up. Professor Hanaa wore nothing but a pale blue hospital gown tied at the back. It was an impersonal gown, lacking in colour, form and personality. She knew she was pale and that her face was full of wrinkles. She felt totally impotent, fatigued and emaciated. Her femininity was pushing her into an abyss of darkness and despair.

The nurse propped Hanaa's back with a strong hand but without the slightest tenderness. She got up with difficulty, hugging her belly in her arms, as if hiding her grief and defeat.

He turned his head suddenly and looked at her. She tried to stand up and hold herself upright, then leaned fully on the nurse's arm.

He was rooted to his place for a few moments, his eyes lingering on her face, on her body, on her arms.

He looked at the hospital gown, and the drops of blood which left their traces on the gown, and even on the floor. Her blood was stealthily escaping from her like a practised robber.

He moved suddenly, without thinking. He bent over, pulled out a Kleenex from his pocket and wiped the blood trickling down her leg. He put his arms around her strongly and told the nurse, 'You go. I'm her husband.'

The nurse nodded without the slightest trace of surprise, let go of Hanaa and left.

Hanaa did not raise any objections, as if her strength had abated for good. He opened the bathroom door and whispered in her ear, 'What do you need?'

Barely able to breathe, and with a touch of panic, she said, 'I'm OK. Just exhausted. And I've lost a lot of blood. You shouldn't see me like this, shouldn't see my blood like this, or be here, or hold me, or stay with me – I don't need you. Nor—'

She swallowed hard, took a deep breath and fell silent.

He went into the bathroom with her, then held her again, propping her back up with his arm until she reached the bed. He helped her lie down, while she felt as if she had crossed the ocean in a few seconds. He bent down again and started wiping the drops of blood she had lost. She stared at him in horror and amazement, then asked, 'Why are you doing this?'

He answered simply, 'I don't know.'

She said suddenly and vehemently, as if she now understood everything, 'Yes. You wanted me weak and helpless. You need me when I'm weak. You hated me when I was stronger than you. But you love me when I'm weaker than you.'

Holding her hand firmly he said, 'Maybe.'

'That's the truth.'

Sitting down beside her he said, 'Of course you know everything. And I should not oppose you, or else …'

She knew he wanted to take her in his arms, and she did not object. Why should she?

He tenderly pulled her close and put her head on his chest, tenderness gushing forth from his heart as it had never done before. Her hand pressed into his shoulder and she whispered, 'This is so much better. I didn't want to be a single mother. Now I can focus on my work. This traitor of a womb was always a problem, but now it's dead and gone. It's no longer part of me. Tomorrow you'll marry someone else, have children and work. And I don't want to see you ever again, Khaled. Ever. I will live for my work. I have nothing else left.'

His fingers moved through her hair, which was wet with the sweat of the exhausting trip to the bathroom. He pondered, 'I get married, and you dedicate your life to knowledge. Is that what you want?'

She said with conviction, 'Yes. That's the reasonable thing to do.'

'What if I dedicated my life to knowledge, and you got married?'

She looked at him reproachfully, turning away from him. 'This is not a time to joke.'

'I'm just asking. Seems to me to be the reasonable thing to do.'

'Your kind of reason is always different from mine.'

'I have no reason left, professor. You murdered my reason the day you seduced me and gave me a gift I had not asked for.'

'Nor wanted.'

'Why did I take it then? Come on, professor. Put your head back on my chest. We listen to reasonable things all the time on the radio and on television. Reasonable things are constantly being dictated to us by those who are stronger and wealthier than we are.'

She put her head back on his chest, and suddenly whispered weakly, 'Now what do you feel? Pity? Love? No, I'm sorry. Sometimes I behave like a little naïve girl asking silly questions. I want to sleep.'

He put her head on the pillow and put his arm under her head as if she were his child. He lay down beside her and whispered, 'I love you, Professor Hanaa. I love you.'

He kissed her brow, and whispered again, the words soothing him. He repeated them to himself, more than telling them to her. 'And I want you. No one else. I don't care about the world. I've lost my mind, my dreams, my life. I now want only you.'

She did not speak. She smiled calmly, held his hand and pulled it close to her heart. She hugged it, and closed her eyes.

With a touch of sarcasm he whispered, 'You don't believe a word of what I am saying, do you?'

She shook her head. 'Never mind.'

She placed his hand on her heart, curled up as she always did, and whispered, 'Tomorrow you'll forget. Tomorrow you'll get married, and I will live for my work ... and knowledge ... and ...'

His fingers glided through her clammy hair again, and he said, 'Of course, tomorrow you'll live for your position, you'll change the world and you'll bring dignity and justice to a people used to corruption and oppression. But now you'll sleep in my arms. Tomorrow Egypt will see a new era of democracy at your hands, Professor Hanaa. Good night.'

He heard her breath becoming even and felt her hand relaxing. She fell into a deep sleep.

He remained quiet, close to her. He only wanted to be close to her. Amidst all the impersonal things in the room, there were only the two of them. In a dull world that had lost its individuality, she was to him the sum of all colours and shapes and feelings, and he was to her the epitome of happiness, and sadness and despair. Tubes were stuck to her arms, like all the patients in the hospital. She had been the first woman in his life, and he was the first man in her life. Together they had learned the meaning of intimacy, of deceitfulness, of war and of conflicts. Now, amid all this medical equipment, the torment and the pain, he wanted to be with her, close to her, nothing more.

The nurse opened the door and said, 'I'm sorry, sir. You can't stay in the room overnight.'

He smiled, 'Where are you from?'

'Boulaq.'

'We're neighbours, then.'

He sat up, then got to his feet. He put his hand in his pocket, pulled out twenty pounds and asked, 'What's your name?'

'Nawal. But it's against regulations—'

He interrupted her, slipping the twenty-pound note into the pocket of her white coat, and said, 'We're from the same neighbourhood, Nawal. Just for today.'

She nodded hesitantly, then said, 'All right. But please don't leave the room. If anyone were to see you —'

'I won't till the morning.'

He smiled, feeling relieved. Then he took Hanaa in his arms again.

If she found out that he had bribed the nurse, she'd reprimand him. But she would never understand that Nawal didn't do this just for the twenty pounds, but to help him, too. She would not understand that bribes were not always paid by a villain to a villain. In Egypt, bribes were mostly given by one of the oppressed to another.

He was not willing to let go of her. Not now, nor ever before. No, he was not willing to let her write history. From the start he had relentlessly sought to pluck the pen from her hand. The doorman had his phone number, and Khaled had told him to inform him promptly of everything that happened to her. He had not been willing to give her the chance to write again, ever. He did not like what she wrote. He didn't like it, nor want it.

In the morning she opened her eyes to find herself in his arms: he was declaring full control over her. He smiled, propping her up, and said, 'Good morning, darling.'

He had never used 'darling' before. He was different, and he was pining for her. He tried to seem normal, and to appear in control of his emotions. She felt pride welling up in her, which she, too, sought to hide. It was a sense of pride she did not understand, a sense of pride because of the effect she had on him.

Feeling reassured, she asked, 'How did you manage to sleep at the hospital?'

'I have my illegal methods!'

She smiled, her eyes following him while he first opened the window overlooking the street, then the window opening on to the light shaft. He was not worried about the mouse; he knew it would find its way amidst the rubbish. He knew the mouse would survive.

He asked her eagerly, 'What would you like for breakfast?'

She whispered weakly, 'Nothing.'

He held her wrist, and said tenderly, 'You must eat. A lot. Look at your wrist!'

She answered in a monotone, holding her belly, 'Khaled, aren't you going to the university today?'

'No. I'm staying with you.'

She opened her mouth to object, then closed it again. She needed him with her; she wanted him with her.

The doctor entered with an air of indifference, looked at Khaled in surprise and asked, 'Who is this?'

She smiled proudly, held his hand and declared, 'My husband.'

The doctor took her pulse, prescribed some painkillers, then left.

He played tenderly with her hair, and asked, 'Are you in pain?'

She felt her abdomen, and a deep sense of sadness rolled over her again. 'A bit.'

'What about some *kunafa*?'

'What?!'

'You need a lot of sugary stuff. Some baklava then?'

'I don't like —'

'Doesn't matter. This is therapy,' he interrupted.

'Therapy with pastries?'

'The best form of therapy.'

Getting up from the bed and moving towards the door, he said, 'I won't be long.'

She answered impulsively, 'Don't be late. Don't be late, Khaled.'

She kept glancing at the clock on the wall, awaiting his return. She tried not to think of the pain. What would have happened if he had not found out about her admittance to hospital? What if he had known but had not come to see her? She had expected to go through the loss and pain on her own. Now she was not sure if she would have been able to. All her courage, freedom and independence had vanished with the first blow of pain tearing at her guts. If there was one human being in the whole world she wanted to be beside her, it was Khaled. Just Khaled.

When he returned, he looked at her again as he was standing in the door. He frowned. The truth suddenly struck him: she was in hospital, hovering between life and death; there were all these tubes and painkillers, all this fatigue and pain on her face. Amazingly, she now clung to him. And it wasn't a pretence. He knew it was genuine; he sensed it.

He walked in and came to the bed. He sat facing her, but avoided her eyes. 'Look what I bought you,' he said enthusiastically.

She smiled, and said in exhaustion, as the effect of the painkiller was receding, 'What did you buy?'

'Pastries, chips, *kofta* and kebab, playing cards, books, milk—'

She interrupted him as the pain started taking over. 'Why don't you look at me? Why do you hardly look at me?'

He didn't answer, but said enthusiastically, 'Eat first, then drink a lot of milk.'

She bit her lip so as not to scream, and whispered, 'Please go out, Khaled. Please.'

He looked at her, held her hand and said, 'I'll call the doctor, Hanaa.'

She screamed in pain.

Panicking and trying to free his hand from her grip, he said, 'Hanaa. I'll call the doctor.'

He was about to get up, but she grabbed him. Clinging to him, she said in confusion, 'Don't leave me.'

He said straight away, 'I'll just call the doctor. I won't leave you.'

He left feeling strained, and went in search of the doctor, while Hanaa rang the bell for the nurse.

He returned after a few minutes and sat down beside her on the bed while she held her belly as if crushing it. 'He's coming, Hanaa. He'll be here in a few minutes.'

She was breathing slowly, as if suppressing a scream. She closed her eyes, and opened her palm for him. He took hold of her hand, smiled warmly and tried to distract her from her pain. 'I heard you replaced me with a cat!'

She smiled in spite of the agony she was in and said, 'The cat hasn't eaten in two days, Khaled.'

'Darling, if you ask me to take care of your cat while you are in hospital, I'll kill her! Don't, my dear. The competition between us is too strong.'

She smiled again, and whispered, 'You are better than the cat.'

'Thanks for the compliment.'

She opened her mouth to speak, but he whispered, 'Close your eyes, and don't think of the pain. He'll be here in a few minutes.'

When the doctor came, he gave her some painkillers.

A few minutes later she said timidly, averting her face, trying to sleep, 'I'm sorry. I wasn't being myself.'

He was exasperated by her illness, by the hospital, by himself, by everything. He was angry at the world, and said crossly, 'Why are you sorry? Speak up! Scream! You are human! You can feel like humans. It's OK to feel pain.'

She looked at him, long and close, then said in bewilderment, 'Khaled, you're very kind.'

He smiled mockingly. 'Nobody is very kind. Don't put all your trust in me, professor.'

She said slyly, 'Today I trust you. Tomorrow I won't. Will you stay with me? At least for today and tomorrow? Not forever, of course.'

He cupped her small face in his hands, and said in that ironic tone she had missed, 'I'll stay with you. For a day or two. No, not forever, of course.'

He knew what he wanted, and he had known from the start: her. She had turned his life upside down with her aggressiveness, stinginess, selfishness, stubbornness, defiance, haughtiness, reclusiveness, her longing and yearning for him, her weakness, her fear, her nervousness ... in short, all those things which he hated in women.

She was *Professor Hanaa,* not just Safaa or anyone else. She wasn't the type to take care of him or to back him. He mourned the wasted years of his life.

Well then, let her work. Let her pursue success. Let her think of him sometimes, not always. Let her ask him to do the laundry ... no, not to that extent. He would hire a maid and solve the problem. Then they would buy a dishwasher and a washing machine and a tumble dryer, and he wasn't going to care if he didn't find any breakfast in the morning – as long as she was in his arms. Why did a man need a simple woman? What he needed was different. He needed her weakness when she was in his arms, and her strength when she was among people. He didn't know why, but he only wanted her, no one else.

He did not want her to be his boss, though; nor did he want her to dominate him like she always did. He wanted her to be like him, or at least somewhat like him. He wanted her to be a woman who needs a man and who desires a man, one whose weakness he could love and whose strength he could fear.

If he made her fall from power, what could he expect? That she would come back to him mortified?

He was not going to think now. She would become his wife, and the whole world would be told that she was his wife. He would spend the rest of his life fighting her, them, himself. He would be martyred in the heat of the battle against everything ... and he didn't care.

There was a war to be fought with the outside world and another war within. He would win the war with his inner self because he missed her, wanted her, adored her, and wasn't thinking. He was mad, and eccentric. He was young, strong and passionately in love; a love no one understood, nor ever would; a love he didn't want to describe.

What if she didn't return to him?

Never. He couldn't even consider the possibility. He just couldn't.

He visited her daily, and each time he stayed with her for most of the day. He hardly did anything else. He would go to university from time to time and listen in silence to the news and rumours that circulated about Professor Hanaa's illness. For some odd reason, those days at the hospital were days of happiness for both. They spent their time together like an old couple, and no one asked about them. There were no expectations, no history, no house, no kitchen, no heirlooms, no carpets, no books ... nothing that bothered either of them. She knew that she would always lovingly remember those white hospital curtains, because he pulled them open every morning, smiling at her innocently, eagerly, lovingly.

Two weeks later she returned home. He remained with her all the time. He still went to university, and still listened to the other professors talking and plotting. He knew what he wanted. He knew he didn't want her to remain the head of the department.

He felt a strange lump in his throat when he measured up her anger, despair and love against each other.

She wanted to deprive him of his livelihood, and others of theirs. He didn't like that. He loved her passionately, but did not want her to be the head of the department. He loved her passionately, but wanted to destroy her dream in a wink.

He did not consider his conflicting emotions, nor did he consider what they might lead to.

***

Samy whispered in his ear, 'Her end is near! God struck her down so that we could get rid of her.'

He swallowed hard, a shiver running down his spine, while a weird sense of hatred and contempt for Samy overwhelmed him.

He said with forced calmness, 'What do you have in mind?'

Samy smiled confidently. 'There are plenty of transgressions that I've discovered.'

He replied with determination, 'She never lapses.'

'True. Her problem is that she goes by the book. That in itself is a transgression. Abdel Hamid has prepared some documents, and we'll go to the Dean—'

He interrupted Samy sharply, 'No. Don't.'

Samy stared at him in bafflement while Khaled contained himself and said again, 'Professor Samy. I think it is better if you don't interfere. Otherwise the Dean might think it is part of a conspiracy. I have another solution.'

'Which is?'

'Give me a chance.'

'Tell me what it is first.'

'You'll see. Just give me two weeks, no more.'

'And if you don't keep your promise?'

He gave him a wry smile. 'Give me a chance, Professor Samy.'

'Why?'

'Why? What?'

'Why do you hate her so passionately?'

He swallowed hard, in distress, then said, 'She jeopardizes my income.'

'Then why not let me handle her?'

He did not reply. Samy looked at him, then said, 'Khaled, I don't understand you. Or perhaps I do understand you. You don't want me to frame her, do you?'

'Exactly.'

'But I wouldn't frame anyone. She did do wrong – she treated Abdel Hamid unfairly. He's already submitted a complaint to the president of the university. She also withheld travel grants from three professors, under the pretext that their scholarly abilities are poor. Then she used the money to buy books for the library – from a friend in the United States, of course. Do you want more? There's the issue with the scholarship—'

Khaled smiled scornfully. 'Professor Samy, these are not the charges that you will take to the Dean.'

'Khaled ...'

'It doesn't matter. Just give me a chance.'

'You're a good lad, Khaled. Dependable and loyal. But you know how to weasel through! You'll have a bright future.'

***

The tears poured down her old wrinkled face. It hurt him, and once again he felt helpless.

She would not talk to him except when it was absolutely necessary. She spent most of her time cursing his wife, and at all other times she would sob and cry uncontrollably.

He got up in determination, took his mother's hand and pleaded, 'Mum, please come with me.'

She followed him resignedly, still cursing his wife.

He heard his sister shouting, 'How could you do this to your own mother? What for – for a woman? She's not worth it, Khaled. You've got duties and your place in society. You have duties towards your mother and your sister and—'

'Shut up!' he interrupted her decisively.

Then he looked at his sister, trying to fathom why she tormented him incessantly. He couldn't fully grasp the reason for his sister's commitment to ruining his life.

He sat on the bed in his room, facing his mother, and said, 'I can't. I simply can't. Every person has a limit. Even God only burdens the believer with what he can bear. Don't order me to do something I cannot do. You're my mother.'

She shouted through her tears, 'She's just a female, nothing more, nothing less. Whether a professor or not, she's just like any other woman. Do you really want to sell your mother for a woman, my son?'

He replied calmly, 'I would never sell you. But she's my wife now. It's too late to leave her.'

Furious she replied, 'You're drooling over her, like those men we hear about. She'll never give you a child. She's not your age and she's not from your social class.'

She fell silent, then asked reproachfully, as if she had just discovered that her son smoked, 'You love her?'

He answered impulsively, 'I want her as my wife. I don't want to divorce her. I want her to be with me.'

'Oh yes, you love her like a teenager. May God punish her and ruin her.'

He had expected these words, and knew them well.

His sister stood in the door and asked defiantly, 'Why are you doing this to us?'

He looked at her sternly and ordered, 'Go to your room, Shaimaa, and close the door.'

His mother shouted, 'Why? She's my girl and worries about me.'

He thought for a moment, then tried again, using all the weapons available to him. 'Mother, I have lived my whole life thinking about what would make the others happy, thinking of duty. I have done what was right for society and for our family; I have put up with responsibilities, poverty, education, you, my father, my brother, my sister. Now there is one thing I need and want. One thing, nothing else.'

'A wrong thing.'

'What's wrong about my wife?'

'She can't have children.'

'I don't want anyone else.'

'You'll be sorry when it's too late.'

'Maybe. We'll see about the regret.'

'She's just a woman. Why her?'

The conversation kept reverting to the same point again and again.

'I don't know. I want her. Please. Just give me this one chance to live for myself.'

She opened her mouth, but he hurriedly said, pulling a key out of his pocket, 'This is the key to the flat in al-Haram Street which I bought. It's yours.'

She asked in surprise, 'Aren't you going to live with your wife in it?'

He answered firmly, 'It's yours. And I have another surprise, too. I have booked you a trip to Mecca for the lesser pilgrimage this year; next year, God willing, I will book you a for *Hajj*.'

She took the key and held it, saying with a touch of anger, 'You think I want your money. You think I'm after your money.'

'Of course not. This is my duty, Mum.'

She answered stubbornly, 'But I don't want her living in this house. Or to use you any more than she already does.'

He gave no answer, but reflected for a few moments. Then he found the ideal solution.

He said calmly, 'But I don't love her. Of course not. And she doesn't use me.'

She looked at him in surprise, so he went on hurriedly, 'On the contrary. I need her to get my PhD. Otherwise, I'll never get it. I just need her, and I'm at ease with her. Who said that I love her? As you said, she's just a woman. Of course I don't love her.'

She sighed, wiping away her tears, then said, 'Will you come visit us? Or will you forget your mother?'

'Every day. I'll visit every day.'

'And what about her? Will she visit us?'

Getting to his feet, he answered, 'It doesn't matter. She's not important. Why should she visit you?'

She replied jealously, 'You're going to her, like always, and you'll leave us.'

He whispered tenderly, 'She's sick. I can't leave her. Shall I go to her, or would you rather I brought her to live with you here? Or in the flat in al-Haram Street?'

She answered hurriedly, 'Go to her.'

He hugged her, she kissed him and he kissed her. She asked him to have lunch with her – and this was her declaration of control over him, and his pledge of endless love for her.

He felt strangely elated at his mother's forgiveness, and had a strong desire to eat some pastries with his mother, his sister and his friend.

He smiled at Muhammad as his mother placed the pastries in front of them, sitting down silently. She was not happy, but she was not angry and tearful; nor did she lay the burden of the world on his shoulders. She did not use her mighty store of weapons, like her power as a mother, or command him to obey his parents or anything of that nature.

Feeling the rim of his plate, as if trying to identify it before he ate from it, Muhammad asked, 'Did you convince her?'

Khaled whispered, exhausted but relieved, 'We're not discussing it.'

Silence prevailed while Muhammad was still feeling his way around the plate of pastries. He felt the sugar sticking to his fingers. It was warm and moist between his fingers.

Then his fingers dipped into a piece of lush crumbly *basbousa*. His fingers loved the feel of pastries, because they gave him a sense of warmth and security. He squeezed the piece of *basbousa* in his hand and felt its feeble pores being crushed, yielding longingly, submissively, despairingly.

Basbousa.

Muhammad didn't want any *basbousa*, though. He wanted some baklava, then some *kunafa*.

He asked Khaled wonderingly, 'Hasn't your mum made us any baklava?'

Khaled smiled. No doubt, he smiled. He seemed happy. He picked up a piece of baklava, held his friend's hand confidently and placed the baklava in it.

Muhammad pressed the piece of fragile baklava. It was fragile yet strong and delicate. He heard its sound as its layers broke in his hand, melted in his mouth. The baklava was much stronger and much harder than the *basbousa*. It felt firm, as if it were layers of ancient papyrus which crumbled as soon as one touched them.

Baklava!

The *kunafa*, however, Muhammad did not like. He could not understand those sticky strands that cling together in fear with an amazing will to survive. The *kunafa*, too, was strong and hard, and Khaled loved it.

Kunafa!

Khaled glanced at his watch and said, 'Let's pray the evening prayer – then I have to go.'

'As long as your mum makes these pastries, I want to live here!'

Khaled got up, his mother following him lovingly and loyally with her eyes. He hugged her again, and then left with his friend in tow.

His mother remained seated, feeling a tinge of sorrow, a tinge of bewilderment. She stared at the key to her son's house, not sure what to do with it.

Her daughter blurted out eagerly, sitting down next to her, 'Mum. She's had a hysterectomy. Didn't you tell me that when a woman has had a hysterectomy, it's her husband's right to take a second wife? Of course he'll leave her. I'm certain he will.'

She looked at her daughter in horror. 'What nonsense is this? That's not acceptable, Shaimaa.'

'You said so. I heard you. He'll leave her soon.'

The mother was silent for a moment, then said, 'Your brother won't leave her. He may never leave her. It's a calamity. These things are created to try our faith. I have to live through it. I'll never see his children for as long as I live.'

Vexed, Shaimaa said, 'He won't leave her? How do you know that? How do you know what's written in the stars?'

'Khaled is my son. I carried him close to my heart for nine months. I know my son. I know how he thinks.'

'How does he think?'

'Don't you see how he treats Muhammad? Khaled is used to helping and shouldering responsibility. He loves taking care of others. But worst of all, he loves her. When a man loves – and when a man like your brother loves – then it's over.'

'What's over?'

'It's over. Now leave me alone. Go study. And don't talk to him any more. Don't you dare talk to him again, or else he'll stop coming here and he'll forget me for good.'

Chapter 9

He had won the first round, but he knew that this was only the beginning of the war, not its end. Still, he didn't care for anything but her. Nothing was going to stand between him and her; not the conflicts, the blame, the oppression, nor all that he was going through and was bound to go through in the future.

He massaged her back as she lay face down on the bed, and whispered, 'Is this better? How do you feel? Does your back still hurt?'

'This pain is almost killing me.'

He continued to massage her, whispering in his usual mocking tone, 'When *you* say that, the pain must be absolutely excruciating.'

'How did it go with your mum?'

'She's fine.'

'I'm not asking about her health, Khaled.'

'What then?'

'How did you convince her? *Did* you convince her?'

'What do you care, if you're planning to leave me anyway? Or have you changed your mind?'

His touch felt tender now on her back, but she said nervously, 'Don't push so hard.'

'I don't.'

'Yes you do. I want to know.'

Pressing hard this time, he replied, 'She likes you. My mother likes you and respects you. She's very happy about our marriage.'

She laughed out sarcastically, 'Very.'

He insisted, 'Very. It was her wish that I marry someone who'd make me happy. That wish has come true.'

She opened her mouth, but he interrupted her, whispering into her ear, 'I want to make love to you again. I miss you. I miss you so much.'

She turned her face and looked at him. Then she stared at the floor, thinking of what he had just said. She felt strangely ashamed of herself, of her weakness and of everything that she had lost, as if it were her fault. Being ill was mortifying and humiliating. And she hated both.

Without any warning her weakness, her femininity, her mortification and nature's control of her – as her sister had said – it all suddenly overwhelmed her. It was the final shove that pushed her into a deep abyss of fear – fear of loneliness, of death, of being in need one day of a hand to prop her up and not finding it.

Her tears finally poured forth freely. She sat on the bed, facing him. Her tears fell, shaking the world around her.

He had not expected this. She had surprised him as she always did. He did not speak or move. Her crying was escalating steadily. It was taking a new form he had not seen before. It confused and scared him.

He whispered in confusion, 'Why?'

She was dashing her tears away impatiently, while the sound of her crying was penetrating the wall. 'I'm OK. It's nothing. Just the hospital and all – and I'm feeling a bit sorry for myself.'

What had always moved him and controlled him was her weakness, affected at times but genuine at others. She was usually strong, but now she was so weak, and it was that which truly worried him, scared him, shook him and even paralysed him.

He was beginning to understand her, her defeat, her helplessness, her timidity, her lack of confidence in her own femininity; but most of all he understood her helplessness.

This feeling of helplessness was the main motivation around them, and was what now brought them close together.

He looked at her, but did not move. He did not console her. He knew the occasional importance of a good cry. He recalled her loneliness, her blood and the loss of something precious.

After a while he held her face in his hands and kissed her several times all over it, whispering in between kisses, 'That's enough, Hanaa. Stop crying, love.'

She nodded, but still sobbed.

He made love to her, and what bonded them was much more than moments of ecstasy. There was a feeling of helplessness, of longing, of fear, of tension, of total intimacy, of mutual understanding, of tenderness, of defiance of everything.

While she throbbed with life around him and her mind seemed to scatter about like drops of water in his arms, her tears flowed heavily. He knew he would never forget these moments.

After they had made love, she moved her fingers across his chest above his heart, as if she were holding a pen and writing invisible words. Her fingers knew their way to his chest and heart, even while her tears still glistened in her eyes.

He whispered in her ears, 'Hanaa. You're the most beautiful woman I've ever set eyes on. And the only one I ever want. Do you understand that?'

She looked at him through her tears. Her fingers trembled for a moment, as if the pen had stopped and was confounded in her hands. Her hand hovered over his heart. Then, as if trying to control the confused pen, she said, 'You just said "Hanaa"! Didn't I tell you before? You said "Hanaa" again! Never take liberties with me!'

He smiled and said, 'I can't focus when I'm with you in the same room ... and the same bed. Excuse me this time.'

Silence prevailed, while her palm throbbed with his heartbeats. Then she said, 'What do you want to happen?'

'Let's not talk about expectations. Talk to me about something else.'

'My brother and sister never bothered to call.'

He answered calmly, 'How can they call when they don't know?'

'They haven't called for months.'

Hugging her closer he said, 'Hanaa – I mean Dr Hanaa – the presence of the cat is making me insecure. Are you sure you want to keep the cat?'

She smiled, 'You're never serious.'

He answered seriously, 'I'm dead serious. This is the best time to ask you to get rid of the cat. Or are its services better than mine?'

She whispered, flirtatiously kissing his shoulder, 'Khaled—'

He asked seriously, 'Are you going to tell me "I love you more than the cat, Khaled?"'

'Stop worrying about the cat.'

'And you'll never say "I love you, Khaled?"'

'Never.'

'I knew it. This is the Professor Hanaa I know. Now I don't need to worry about you any more.'

He sensed her bruised spirit, and the existence of a part in her that he could not reach, in the depths of her femininity, no matter what he did to ease the bruises. He loved her every day, forcefully, fearfully, defeated and with a sense of guilt which often vanished rapidly.

She was either his lover or his boss. She could not be both. And he did not dare to make her choose. He feared that if he made her choose, she would choose to remain his boss, when he could not leave her. Ever since he was a child, he was convinced that the history of Egypt was impossible for him to write, because his pen was not fit to write it; but writing his personal history was his duty. He had always been in control of his fate, and wrote his own history defiantly. His relationship with the government may be the relationship of ruler and subject, but his relationship with others was one of power and authority.

He was pained by her constant worries about her post even while she was ill. She would enquire from time to time, 'What are they up to? Why doesn't the Dean call me? I have to go back to work.'

And he would always reply, 'Think of your health and yourself.'

For some reason she did not go to work. All her energy was focused on him, was spent on talking to him for hours on end, on waiting for him, on embracing him. He was happy about this sudden change, because he had always hoped for a change like this.

And yet he was torn apart by a conflict the like of which he had never experienced before: he wanted her, but he also wanted to dethrone her.

He had to plan carefully and consider all the angles and possibilities.

When he left for work on Saturday morning, he knew that he would see Professor Samy in the University Hall. He knew that Professor Samy had tired of waiting and that if he did not act soon, she would be dismissed from her post as Head of the Department in scandal, charged with a misdemeanour.

He had made up his mind, and stood there waiting to see the Dean.

The Dean looked at him through his small glasses, then asked, 'How are you, Khaled?'

He answered in a calm but lifeless tone, 'I'm fine.'

'You came to talk to me about something important?'

'Yes, about Professor Hanaa.'

The Dean answered derisively, 'Everyone is talking about Professor Hanaa. Do you, too, want Professor Maysah to become the head?'

He replied confidently, 'Yes.'

The Dean got to his feet, saying, 'I'll think about it.'

'She's my wife.'

He stared at Khaled for a few seconds, as if he had not heard him, then said, 'The rumour that reached me said so, but I couldn't believe it. She is too careful. She would never do something like that. And you – why did you come to me with that?'

He answered truthfully, 'Because I know that she will be framed, and that the charges brought against her, although untrue, will ruin her!'

The Dean answered sarcastically, 'So you've decided to take matters into your own hands! You want to ruin her before they do.'

'Being my wife will not ruin her reputation, but being labelled corrupt and a thief will.'

The Dean smiled calmly. 'The reasoning of a man. What can I say? A man who wants a woman to himself, to clip her wings so she forgets how to fly. Do you love her? Of course you do! What else? Does she jeopardize your livelihood?'

Khaled felt very uncomfortable listening to the Dean exposing him in this way.

The Dean went on contemplating, as if he had just watched a farcical play. 'This woman is a weird creature. She used to follow every law and regulation to the letter, and was blindly devoted to the university. Then what? She goes and secretly marries a student of hers, a student whose supervisor and boss she is. Where is her academic integrity?'

Khaled was about to defend her, but the Dean interrupted him. 'I know of course. Hanaa was never easy to deal with or to understand. There is nothing more dangerous than a woman you can't understand!'

The Dean paused, then went on. 'Fine, Khaled. Have it your way. You have a marriage certificate, I presume? But I don't need it. Thank you, Khaled.'

He left the room half dazed, half suffocating.

He did not return home. What if the Dean were to call her now? What if she needed him? What if she cried, and—

No. He would not think of that. She was strong, and would survive it. She wanted him, and would not leave him!

She had lost everything. What had he done to help her? He despised himself for a moment, then he sighed, feeling extremely fatigued. He never helped her. He didn't help her.

He buried his head in his hands, sitting in the junior staff room, breathing in the dust of chalk, of old books, of mothballs; but he did not go home.

What had he done? How would she react? No – he was not going to feel sorry. He wanted her, and she knew it.

Yes, she would forgive him. He would love her as he yearned to. He would make it up to her. He would overwhelm her, strangle her, be her death!

A tear died in his throat.

He stayed put, as if his senses had become numb. He did not move for what seemed like hours.

In his mind's eye he once more saw that little mouse in the hospital light shaft amidst the rubbish, the mould, the old wall, the darkness. He did not know how long the mouse would live. How sorry he had felt for that mouse! How sorry he had felt for its naïve determination to survive! It jumped about, disappeared, dodged, hid, suddenly reappeared and ran.

It exuded life, its limbs delicate and resilient, tiny and pale. Its body was filthy, and its grubby tail was stroking its way over everything with carelessness and audacity.

What would happen if it escaped? Where would it go?

Would it always have to live amidst the rubbish, with the relics of the past, the remains of poverty?

Did the mouse have a way out?

It was safe in the dark light shaft. Outside the light shaft it would be hungry and lost. No doubt, it would be dead.

The darkness gave it a sense of security; history gave it a sense of warmth.

The mould gave it a sense of ease, and the rubbish a sense of stability. The old wall gave it a sense of trust in tomorrow: a sense of trust that tomorrow would inevitably come, as the wall was inevitably permanent, as life was inevitably wasted, as he was inevitably doomed to be defeated.

He stayed put, as if his senses had become totally numb and wouldn't allow him to move.

He heard his friend's footsteps. He needed him!

Sitting down beside him, Muhammad said, 'Poor Professor Hanaa.'

Khaled remained silent.

'This is a country that doesn't appreciate academia.'

He did not reply.

'Khaled, what's wrong?'

He whispered hoarsely, 'I don't know what I've done. I think I've broken her. And I don't know how to fix what I've broken.'

Muhammad was puzzled and asked, 'Why did you break her?'

'You know why.'

'You want her for yourself?'

'Certainly. And I didn't have the guts to give her the choice.'

'You never give anyone any choices.'

'Do you think she'll take me back?'

Muhammad exclaimed sarcastically, 'Do I think she'll take you back? Do I think she'll take you back? No. Of course not. But there is still Safaa.'

He answered nervously, 'I haven't done anything.'

'I said there is still Safaa.'

'Why do you say that?'

'What do you want me to say?'

'Just that she'll take me back.'

'She'll take you back.'

'Tell me the truth! Do you think she'll take me back?'

'Why don't you go home and find out for yourself?'

He got up impulsively and said, 'Yes. I should go home.'

He did not go home, though. He sped off in his car to the pyramids in the dark of the night. He knew he would not be able to get too close to the pyramids.

No. He would not be able to get much closer.

The poverty and misery of the shacks along both sides of the desolate dirt road did not draw his attention. The poverty, in particular, he did not see. He was one of these people, and he knew them. He had shared in their deprivation and poverty all his life. He felt comfortable among them, even though he was now much better off, because he was still one of them. He had been the lucky one, that was all. What really drew his attention was a big billboard amidst all this poverty. It was mounted on the façade of an ugly building, like a frail giant, and said, 'If you dream, we'll make your dreams come true!'

He smiled in dejection at the giant, the advertisement, and the company that had selected poverty and misery as an ideal location for this display of trade and wealth.

What did that company sell? He did not know. What were the dreams it was going to fulfil? He did not know.

He looked at the Great Pyramid from afar.

That was enough. The pyramids always inspired him with a sense of confidence and comfort.

Damn these hard times we live in and what they do to people!

Had he been wrong because he wanted to seize the leadership? To grab the pen and write himself? Did he have to remain a bystander forever? Who in Egypt held the pen? Who wrote? Who controlled everything? Like the rest of them, he was getting used to resigning himself to the dirty grains of sand strewn into his eyes.

Like the rest of them, he did not interfere in what was none of his concern. Nor did he attempt to change anything.

Like the rest of them, he capitulated to the decision-makers. He allowed the winds to blow him about, as Abdel Halim's song said.

At the whims of the winds, they blow, the winds, they blow!
I plod and plod along, I have to bow!

All this was part of his Egyptianness. His determination, his resignation, his patience, his passion were all part of his Egyptianness.

At a time when he failed to move his hand to wipe the dust out of his eyes, his environment, his neighbourhood, his university or even his country, at a time of absolute helplessness and despair as old as history, he was but a man who longed for a woman and wanted to write their history together. Was it fair that someone else should hold the pen?

While his life was shaped by others and his character depicted, reflected and criticized by others, and his life surrounded by glass panes that held him captive but were indestructible, he wanted to be the only one to control that pen. He wanted his own personal happiness.

Right now he was no more than an Egyptian about whom some people wrote. Others demanded his rights from pulpits or platforms or thrones, but no one listened to him, and no one knew him.

He had become an Egyptian – whose flaws are dictated by others and who is forced to sign them off without even reading them over.

Since the dawn of history, he has become used to resigning himself to defeat, despair and cynicism.

But Khaled was different. He wanted to fulfil at least his own personal dreams, if he could not fulfil his national dreams!

Khaled wanted one woman. He was patient but defiant. He enjoyed the fortitude of the ancient Egyptian who had built the pyramids to glorify another, who had borne the heavy stones for ages for the sake of a simple life and morsels of bread.

His wishes were simple, and he felt no regret. Why should he?

Now he had to go home. Yes. He had to go home.

Chapter 10

He swallowed hard. Sorrow was stinging at his eyes and his ears. His eyes reddened with tears and he had to close them for a second. It seemed like it took a lifetime rather than half an hour to get home. Maybe she would not get to know today. Maybe the Dean would not tell her today. Why was he so worried?

He dragged his feet, his heart heavy. He felt no regret. No; no regret. He unlocked the door and went inside.

She was sitting in a big chair in the hall. She looked at him, and their eyes met. Seeing the deep sorrow lurking in her eyes made him blink for a moment. She might burst into tears or explode in his face: he would know in a minute. He opened his eyes and went over to her chair, but Hanaa remained motionless.

He crouched on the floor in front of her, taking her hand between his, and whispered, 'Hanaa ...'

He fell silent for a moment then continued, 'There were a number of conspiracies against you. They wanted to frame you. If I hadn't done it, Professor Samy would have. Do you understand?'

She remained silent.

In despair, he kissed her palm and murmured, 'I haven't had a minute's regret, not a minute. They wanted to get rid of you by creating a scandal. Because of the grant, the Dean himself wanted to get rid of you.'

Turning her face away, she said with feigned indifference, her voice hoarse, 'I am still head of department till Tuesday, when I hand in my resignation.'

He nodded, but did not say a word.

In the same tone she said, 'And Salma will not get the grant.'

He looked at her in amazement: he had not expected such strength at a moment like this.

Snatching away her hand, she said hurriedly, 'He gave me the choice between exposing my marriage to my students and having me up before the board, or my resignation. He would of course expose my marriage, so I had to resign – but Salma will not get the grant, and neither will Muhammad. Ibrahim will get it; he deserves it.'

Earnestly he replied, 'Yes, he's good, and he's committed and he deserves it!'

She looked at him with a bitter smile and hissed quietly, 'You were my Achilles' heel. Everyone has a weak spot. My sister always says a woman is driven by her nature, by her weakness. And you are my weakness.'

He did not utter a word. He got up and stood next to her chair avoiding her eyes, in total silence.

'You, of course, are helpless. You made sacrifices for me and shattered what it took me a lifetime to build.'

Adamantly he said, 'That's not all you built.'

Her voice suddenly loud, she burst out, 'Do you think you're what I built? Is that what you think? That I built this relationship! That I care about this relationship! That I want this relationship?'

'Calm down first, Hanaa,' he said angrily.

'I am very calm.'

She stretched out in the chair, crossed her legs and said with feigned calmness, 'You, my dear Khaled, are the most treacherous man I have ever set eyes on! You come from a lowly environment where women are slaves to men. You, Khaled, are unable to fathom that a woman is a human being. You—'

He interrupted her sternly, 'That's enough, woman.'

She smiled triumphantly and got up screeching, 'To you I am just a woman, nothing more! And to me you are ... you are ...'

She stopped as though panting, then burst out at the top of her voice, 'A lowly coward. A traitor.'

She could feel her voice getting hoarse; her whole body was trembling. She was filled with fury to the very bottom of her soul.

She sank into the chair, her body on fire.

He looked at her; he, too, was seething with rage. He picked up a cup from the table and flung it against the wall. At this point, he was ready to sacrifice all the cups in Egypt rather than slap her.

For a moment, she was shocked, and a shiver ran down her spine.

Then she pulled herself together again.

He bent over the chair she was seated in, leaning on its arms as though trying to trap her. He drew closer and in a voice as quiet as a bomb just before it explodes, he said, 'Don't you dare! Don't you dare ever speak to me like that!'

She stared at him, but she was not afraid of him; she fixed her eyes on his without batting an eyelid. They eyed each other like snakes on the alert, sensing danger. She looked into his eyes and saw her own reflection in his pupils; she saw herself being crushed beneath his feet. He shattered, crushed, drowned her; turned her into a soggy piece of paper with faded letters, of no value.

She had been waiting for this moment, she knew it would come.

He was a Middle Eastern man, a male, one of the common people, vulgar and ... now he was declaring his total dominance over her, talking to her from his lofty position while she was left insignificant, at his mercy, subject to his wishes.

She looked at him briefly with something like disgust, then averted her eyes and said indifferently, 'Go on, hit me, Khaled.

What are you waiting for? I'm a woman, I'm weak and stupid, and I need to be disciplined. You're a man, you shoulder responsibilities and stab people in the back.'

Still looking at her, still bending over the chair, he replied in a voice that was cold and filled with anger. 'I have often imagined myself hitting you. Someday I might, I don't know. I do know that the day I do I'll shatter something that I'll later regret. Right now, the idea is tempting to me like never before. Yes, you're just a woman, nothing more; and you need some disciplining – a lot of disciplining.'

It was obvious that she wanted to break him, to triumph over him. She smiled scornfully.

'This is why I hate men and marriage. Some man leans over me and dictates his conditions like a tyrant, and woe betide me if I don't agree to them.'

He let go of the arms of the chair and turned away from her. She went on, 'You're sick; you and the likes of you are sick. Weakness runs deep in your bones. If you want to hit me, do it now. You already destroyed everything when you stabbed me in the back.'

Slowly, as though carving each word on to his face, she added, 'It's all over between us.'

'OK,' he said with a shrug of indifference.

He stomped off to their bedroom, violently tore the door open, then slammed it shut. He started to get his things together and put them in his bag, anger still burning his eyes, his ears, his heart!

Filled with a rage she had never experienced before, she went after him to the room, opened the door and screamed, 'Don't you close the door like that. If you break it, you'll pay for it.'

He looked at her, feigning calmness. 'How much does the door cost?'

If there was ever a time when she wished to kill him, it was now.

'Your life itself wouldn't pay for it,' she hissed.

Closing his bag he challenged her, 'Shall I break it then so you can kill me? Is that what you want?'

She took a deep breath, as though she had gone crazy and was seeking to exert some self-control. 'You will not get your PhD as long as there is breath left in my body. I'd rather die.'

He did not respond.

He headed for the door. Following him, she screeched, 'Coward ... traitor ... coward ... You wanted to leave me, didn't you? You knew I was going to leave you, or did you think I would stay with you because I lost everything? Did you think I was going to be your slave, gazing daily at you in admiration and awe the way your mother, your sister and everyone else around you does?'

He opened the apartment door. 'How I hate you now!' she screamed, 'and don't you dare slam the door. I'll kill you if you do!'

He slammed the door.

She headed for it burning with rage; she punched the door with a force she didn't know she was capable of.

The tears rolled down her cheeks.

She did not deserve this. She, who in a moment of weakness had let this man into her life.

Her mind went back to years gone by, when she was a twenty-year-old girl in her prime, to the serene love she had had for a young man without knowing anything about him, without asking who he was. Ramy.

If he had been a Muslim, if he had been of the same religion, would he have married her?

He always said, 'A ship can have only one skipper, and the skipper is the man. The woman is the deckhand.'

She had not liked what he had said then, but she liked his serenity and timidity; and she had never felt like she wanted to tear him limb from limb.

Ramy had never pushed her back to the wall and scattered her like dust in the wind.

Their feelings for each other had been serene.

Did she have to accept defeat silently?

Tomorrow.

She looked at the expensive Persian carpet in the hall where she was sitting. She gazed at the colours and patterns. It seemed as if no one had ever come into her life.

Yes, as if no one had come into her life.

Tomorrow she would start anew.

She spied the pastries he had left on the table. Rising from her seat, she picked them up disdainfully, made her way to the kitchen and dumped them in the rubbish bin.

'Idiot.'

She wiped her hands, but could not get rid of the syrup, which stuck to her fingers.

She washed her hands irritably, went to her bedroom, and for the first time in years she lay on her bed fully dressed.

She could feel his scent on the bed; she smelt him on the sheets, on all the furniture.

She should change the sheets. The whole house! Yes, she ought to do that, or go and work abroad. She was sick of Egypt and its honourable men!

What did she have now?

A cat called Basbousa.

She had to change its name immediately or get rid of the cat!

In the span of just one year she had lost an awful lot! Her womb, her heart, her position, perhaps her reputation: an awful lot.

What did she have left other than her graceful wrists, a few research papers and an apartment? She would demand her mother's jewellery.

Yes.

What had she gained?

Nothing. She had lost her virginity; that of course was a benefit.

Nothing, save the sense he had aroused within her, the annoying sense of her femininity. Was it worth all the sacrifice, the humiliation, the degradation?

What more could she lose? She had not much left. What more would she lose?

She felt suffocated. She had to get out quickly.

She walked along the banks of the Nile in the cold night.

She sat facing the Nile. The river seemed cold and calm and deep. She hated its depth and its coldness. She closed her eyes. When she looked at her watch, it was two o'clock in the morning. She had to go back home or else – what would people expect of her if she did not return home? What would men think if they saw her sitting alone like this on a bench along the Nile? Because she was a Middle Eastern woman, she needed a man to restrain and command her. She needed honey, lots of it, to be stuck where she was forever.

Yes, she needed honey, lots of it, to be stuck where she was forever.

She felt completely lost. So her relationship with Khaled was over. This time it was really over. Yes, of course it was. She looked around her, at the Nile, at the lights of its boats and the people walking along the pier. She looked at a street urchin who was no more than ten, although he had the features of a forty-year-old. His clothes were dirty, his trousers torn, and there was a huge infected wound on his right knee. His face was stony as he begged from the passers-by. She did not know if he would spend the night there or if someone would take him off for a shameful encounter then give him ten pounds to buy cigarettes with.

The street urchin scared her. She was frightened by his need for fast cash, by his urge to spend it immediately.

Hesitantly she looked at the passers-by, while her blood ran unfamiliarly cold in her veins.

A small family passed by in front of her. The father drifted by lazy and disgruntled. The mother was veiled and wore a grey cloak; her two teenage daughters were also veiled, and wore jeans and lipstick.

They passed before her like an apparition, followed by a woman accompanied by her husband and child. The woman was short and fat, and not veiled; round her neck she wore a large cross. Her husband, her child and she herself all had the same discontented expression.

Was everyone around her miserable, then? Was that the human condition?

Her ears caught scattered words, sometimes the sound of laughter.

She remembered Ramy once more. He had been young, hesitant and shy, and she had loved those qualities in him. He had feared his mother and loved pastries.

Then Khaled – Khaled. How she wished he were dead, or drowning in the river before her very eyes calling for help; she would laugh and leave him to drown.

She could see Khaled, tall and slim, with that protruding Adam's apple of his which stuck in her memory like the honey had stuck to her hands. He was pious, and never missed a prayer. She did not know if he was calm or not. She did not know him, and she didn't understand him.

He bore through her, drowned her, crushed her and loved her. And she could not stand him any more.

Khaled also loved pastries and feared his mother!

Egypt! Where are you heading? Where will you escape from me?

What unites us? Where are Ramy and Khaled?

Nothing unites us but our fear of our mothers, and our love of pastries.

And she neither feared her mother nor loved pastries.

She could see the threads of her life fraying while a new society, unrecognizable to her, took her to its bosom. What else? What unites us?

Lack of confidence in the political system ... despair, cynicism, the search for the self.

And she? Who was she? What united her with Khaled?

No, she would not think of that now.

Egypt! Where are you heading? Where will you escape from me this time? Will I find you once again? Whose country are you? Khaled's or Professor Hanaa's?

Ramy's or Hajja Leila's?

Again, confusion, despair and helplessness.

She heard the mobile phone in her bag ringing. She did not want to talk to anyone. Especially not to him!

She took the phone out her of bag, her brain barely functioning, and knowing who it was she said vehemently, 'What do you want?'

'Where are you?'

'Why are you asking?' she screeched hysterically. 'Leave me alone, Khaled! You will not dominate me. Believe me, you won't be able to. Have you ever asked yourself why I never got married in all those years? Don't ask me. Don't try to control me as though you were my father; you're years younger than I am. Just divorce me quietly.'

Firmly he said, 'How many times have you asked for a divorce when you didn't mean it? This time, professor, I will divorce you. But where are you? You're not at home. Why?'

Once again she screamed, 'I don't need anyone to worry about me. I've lived for twenty years without anyone worrying about me.'

Quietly he said, 'Hanaa ... where are you? Just tell me where you are so I can come and divorce you. Isn't that what you want?'

Without thinking, she told him.

He hung up. She knew he would come, because she was a woman and needed a man's protection. Of course he would come. Why? To divorce her?

Because he loved and wanted her?

Loved her! The treacherous idiot. To destroy her, and then to make that claim!

However, he had made no such claim.

But she knew he would.

Or perhaps he would make no claim at all. Maybe he would just divorce her quietly as he said he would.

She heard the whistle of a faraway train, smelt the smoke that comes from everywhere and anywhere blended with the smell of the cold night air.

And what about that volcano which overpowered pen and paper, history and glory, the volcano of emotions that he poured on her face, her body and her heart without thought or mercy.

What else was she going to lose?

The next time his handkerchief would not wipe away her blood. There would be a next time, and many more times after that. She would be alone in the hospital while he would be blessed with a wife, children and a happy future ... after he had destroyed her dreams and shattered her life.

She would relieve him of the heavy burden that lay on his shoulders and of that ever-impotent, -fearful and -troubled love.

She would listen to sad tunes, read world literature and publish papers. Perhaps someone in a faraway country would read them without knowing who she was. They might not even know if Hanaa was a male or a female name.

She would bury herself in academia. Maybe make a fresh start. The position of head of department was hers: she deserved it. The Dean would not be there forever; Samy would die one day, and she was patient.

Yes, now she was thinking calmly and logically.

What else would she lose?

With indifference, life had deprived her of her womb as if it were a piece of rotten meat forgotten in the fridge by some woman before she migrated to the New World.

Khaled ...

She closed her eyes and her helplessness surged to the surface. Khaled. In a split second, all logic evaporated and in its place was hatred, anger, despair and vulnerability.

He was gentle, an angel. He sometimes understood her before she spoke and he often sensed her fear and despair, and skilfully and efficiently wiped them away with his handkerchief.

But no! He wasn't an angel. But he would live in peace. He would forget her and she would battle on. What for?

What she had lost was hard to regain.

In a country to which she had given her undying allegiance like a loyal slave, she had reaped nothing but defeat.

Would everything just go on uneventfully as if nothing had happened?

Would she remain looking on in silence and frustration while the rest of her life dwindled away, or would she await the day when her blood would once again flow?

Or would she get her revenge on everybody?

What else would she lose?

The great loss had broken her but it had not deprived her of her strength and her awareness.

No.

She had once asked Ramy, 'Dare I dream?' His answer had been 'No'.

Perhaps he had been right.

Who dared dream in a country that had discovered the secret to mummification and was proud of the discovery?

Khaled did. He dared to dream, to love, to battle and challenge, to stab in the back, to be victorious and to accept defeat, to use every form of weaponry and shield.

Khaled dared to do anything and everything.

Was that what had attracted her to him? His silence and shyness, his challenging manner, the mystery, the false surrender and the patience. The endless patience.

Would she allow him to live in peace after everything he had done to her?

He would sleep well at night, get married, work in a Gulf country, have children and provide for them. His wife would obey him submissively; she would support him and give and give. She would help him take off his jacket, reverently and respectfully dust it down as though it were the World Cup, then kiss it passionately and place it in the cupboard.

That was impossible.

It would never happen!

This was her last defeat.

As usual, she sensed his presence before she even saw him.

She felt his breath, his hand on the back of the bench and a shiver ran down her spine. She was not sure if it was a shiver of hatred or of longing, or both. She did not want to know.

Suddenly he whispered gently, 'Hanaa ...'

'Professor Hanaa,' she corrected him sternly.

He said emphatically, 'No. Just Hanaa. Hanaa, the woman.'

She smiled coldly, 'The woman you stripped of her authority.'

He gazed at the Nile and said, 'I have no regrets. It's a better ending than most. You gave up your position while you were at the top. Would you rather Samy framed you for something and you left university under a dark cloud? I believe you are a professor, a successful one at that, and a great scholar – which is much more important than an administrative position that you'll lose one day. Do you get what I mean?'

'You did what you did because you have no self-confidence, because you—'

He interrupted her. 'I did it because you were interfering in everything, depriving me and others of our livelihood, because you wanted to destroy a thousand-year-old system and you wanted to do it in a year – a system that came into being with Ramses, and you wanted to destroy it. A system we were all brought up on. Do you understand what I mean? You wanted justice and equality to reign, but that is impossible. I tried many times to make it clear to you that it would be better not to change the system but rather to help those who need help. We are a country that loves corruption, conceit, favouritism and especially doing favours for relatives and neighbours – but you don't get it. At the end of the day you were harming yourself and the needy around you.'

Bitterly she said, 'Such intelligence! Give me another convincing reason. Why don't you say that you weren't comfortable with me as your boss?

'Of course,' he burst out. 'Of course, I wasn't comfortable with you as my boss.'

She smiled mockingly, triumphantly and did not speak.

Putting his arm around her and stroking her arm affectionately, he whispered, 'Hanaa ... I never want to leave you.'

In a tone of bitterness and despair she asked, 'Why? Why don't you leave me? Go and marry someone from your own country, from the Egypt you know.'

Gazing once again at the Nile he whispered, 'Sometimes we can't control our feelings. We are all human, and Egypt is big enough for both of us.'

'It's your country. I don't understand it.'

He didn't speak, and withdrew his arm from her shoulder. In silence, he looked around as though he were waiting for her to speak, to surrender, not sure if she would give him what he wanted.

Was it war, then? He did not want a war. He wanted Professor Hanaa, captive or free. He wanted her. He wanted her, whether she came willingly or by force; in chains he wanted her, fortified with shields he wanted her! In that moment he did not know if she was chained or shielded or both.

Rather angrily he said, 'You don't have to understand everything. So long as you are not in a governmental position you don't have to understand anything you don't already know.'

'I'm not used to not understanding my surroundings.'

'But you haven't understood them for forty years. Why do you want to understand them now?'

With a hint of despair and exhaustion he said, 'Let's go home, Hanaa. I want to take you in my arms and I can't do that here. I want to eat baklava with you.'

'I threw it in the garbage can,' she said spontaneously.

'I knew you'd do that, so I bought some more. It's in the car.'

She gazed at him. The bones of his face, his Adam's apple, the collar of his shirt, his eyes which were brimming with stubbornness, love and antagonism.

She sighed. What more was she going to lose?

Sarcastically she said, 'You were sure I'd go with you.'

'Yes!' he said seriously.

'Absolutely certain.'

'Of course.'

'That I'd go with you and eat baklava and admit defeat?'

'And fight, and challenge me, and try me, and get revenge, and ...'

He fell silent then whispered, 'Help me. Sometimes I need your help to face the world; or maybe I need you to provoke me so I can defy you and insist on the success of our relationship.'

'You're stubborn.'

'Very.'

She knew that she could never leave him: he was her destiny, what remained of her life.

She whispered threateningly, 'Khaled, I told you: so long as there is a breath in my body, you will not get your PhD.'

'As long as you are my supervisor, it doesn't matter,' he said at once.

'I'll destroy your future; you'll see.'

He took her hand and rose, pulling her up with him. 'Destroy it while we are together.'

'Yes, while we are together. I won't leave you. Of course I won't ever leave you to live in peace after what you've done to me.'

She took his hand, their fingers firmly intertwined, as though she planned to hold him captive in the dark prison between her fingers and the corners of her life.

Walking by her side he said, 'No, don't let me live in peace. I cannot live in peace!'

Reem Bassiouney the author of five novels. Her first novel *The Smell of the Sea,* appeared in Egypt in 2005 and was a bestseller. All her novels have multiple editions, and are widespread in the Arab world. Her second novel, *The Pistachio Seller* won the best Arabic translated novel ward in 2009 and came out in English from Syracuse University Press October 2009.

Her novel *Professor Hanaa* which appeared in Arabic in 2008 has also appeared in multiple editions including a government subsidized one. It won the first prize in the Sawiris literary award, the biggest award in Egypt. It was also selected as the only novel to come out in 'reading for all book' series (2010), which is the most prestigious series in Egypt.

OUTERCOURSE

The Be-Dazzling Voyage

CONTAINING RECOLLECTIONS FROM MY

LOGBOOK OF A RADICAL FEMINIST PHILOSOPHER

(BE-ING AN ACCOUNT OF MY TIME/SPACE TRAVELS AND IDEAS

– THEN, AGAIN, NOW, AND HOW)

Mary Daly

Illustrated by Sudie Rakusin

The autobiography of the world's foremost Radical Feminist philosopher and author of classics, *Beyond God the Father* and *Gyn/Ecology*. An imaginative weaving of visionary philosophy and autobiography. An intellectual journey that takes us on a series of quantum leaps through the Four Spiral Galaxies and down into the Realm of the Subliminal Sea.

'An incredible voyage into a Reality where thought expands through a thrilling philosophical narrative. Mary Daly gives us a brilliant book in which she invents a new genre of autobiography.... This is the most fascinating, daring, and intelligent autobiography I have ever encountered.'

– Nicole Brossard

'Mary Daly's wit and brazen inventiveness create a new dimension of imagination and political resistance for women. Here she tells us her story – offering an analysis of memory and how to reclaim it, and an original vision of a new world of possibility for women unafraid. There is insight and inspiration in her repudiation of everything that dulls or hurts or diminishes women – and there is the joy of her adventurer's mind. She is a pioneer fighter for a freedom wider and deeper than we thought possible.'

– Andrea Dworkin

'A shimmering and utterly unique achievement, a portrait of the Radical Feminist philosopher as a child, young adult, and wonderlusting Crone.'

– Jane Caputi

RU 486: Misconceptions, Myths and Morals

Renate Klein, Janice G. Raymond and Lynette J. Dumble

Certificate of Commendation (Non-fiction), Human Rights Award 1991

A controversial book about the new French abortion pill. The authors examine the medical literature on the drug, including its adverse effects. They evaluate the social, medical and ethical implications, including the use of women for experimental research, in particular third world populations, and the importance of women-controlled abortion clinics. The book is excellent case study material for medical, health and women's studies practitioners and students.

The authors are experts in feminist ethics, women's health and medical science.

'The three authors ... do a great public service by describing the medically supervised, drawn out, and frequently painful process in which RU 486 is actually administered. They explain the side-effects, expense, media manipulation, and feminist fantasy about RU 486. In clear prose and carefully documented statements they explain what RU 486 is; how it functions in the body; whom it serves; what its history and adverse effects are; what the long-term ethical, political and social consequences are; and most important, what a better alternative is .... This book won a Certificate of Commendation for a Human Rights Award – understandably so.'

– Shulamit Reinharz, *Disability Quarterly*, USA.